To Stacey
birthday -

From,
Cindy

DOUBLE DANGER

"What are you doing here?" demanded the commissioner.

"Sir?" Andy replied.

"Not you," snorted Saunders. "I can guess you're here trying to build a case on thin air. I mean *her*." He stabbed a finger at Kim. "What is the secretary of my insurance agent doing here comparing notes with the attorney for the opposition?"

Andy's jaw dropped. "A spy?"

"A traitor," accused Saunders.

"I never saw him before in my life," gasped Kim, "and that's the truth."

She turned and fled from two pairs of accusing eyes—and slipped. She clawed at the air as she realized, sickeningly, that she was going to slide right under the rope—and crash on the rocks below. . . .

kim aldrich

miscalculated risk

by
JINNY McDONNELL

**cover by
ARNIE
KOHN**

 ® A WHITMAN BOOK
Western Publishing Company, Inc.
Racine, Wisconsin

contents

miscalculated
risk

1
rule of thumb

"Some people are accident-prone, Kim, but, so help me, you're adventure-prone." Dan Aldrich grinned a bit ruefully at his daughter as they walked from their midtown New York apartment to the subway.

Kim made a face at him, then widened her blue eyes innocently. "I haven't done a thing," she protested.

"The day is young, and we just left home," he said dryly. "I'm sure you'll think of something sooner or later. Probably sooner."

"I'll do my best." She laughed, never dreaming how soon she'd regret her light promise. "Actually, you're my first adventure of the day. It isn't often that a girl has a real live FBI agent escort her on a subway ride to Grand Central Station."

"Let's just make the trip quietly and not attract the attention of millions of people, hm?" he suggested mildly.

Kim heaved an exaggerated sigh. "All right. We'll just melt into the crowd," she assured him. "But what a pity. Think of all those people going to their humdrum jobs. If they knew about you, it would add excitement to their lives. Imagine if they could tell about being in the same car with the agent who—"

The hand under her elbow ostensibly guided her down the stairs and through the turnstile and into a train. The fingers dug in.

"Okay, okay; I get the message." She wouldn't really discuss her father's cases in public. "Togetherness is riding a subway during the rush hour," she gasped as they wedged themselves into the aisle and groped for a strap to share.

That was a safe enough subject and fun to pursue. Twice a day, five days a week, a cast of hundreds of thousands performed in perfect unison, as if they had practiced together all their lives.

Kim watched her fellow passengers as the train lurched out of the station. Amazing! Every head swayed back and forth, back and forth, in precise time, her own included. Every body leaned in the same direction as the train roared into a turn.

For six months, ever since finishing her secretarial course, Kim had been a participant in the drama. She loved being a part of the teeming life of the city, but it struck her as funny, nonetheless.

And now it was time for the finale, the Great Escape. They were hurtled into the caverns of

Grand Central. Brakes screeched. Passengers lurched, regained their balance, and pumped their legs up and down, walking in place. It was ludicrous, because they were packed in solidly, and no one could possibly move forward until the doors opened.

Kim planted herself behind her father, so he could run interference for her when the crowd exploded from its confinement. They were met by an incoming tide of determined thousands.

"Let them out. Let them out," pleaded a guard, trying vainly to hold back the surge with outstretched arms.

It was a losing battle for Kim. Her father was outside, and she was pinned inside.

"Let the little girl out," a burly stranger said, laughing.

He planted big hands on her yellow and brown tweed-clad shoulders and shoved. She shot out like a guided missile—minus one shoe. It was an alligator pump, no less. The pair had cost her almost a week's salary, her first extravagance with her own money.

"My shoe!" she yelped. "Find my shoe!"

Miraculously, someone pitched it out just as the doors closed. She caught it in midair, then waved it in salute. Normally blank-faced New Yorkers, on the train and on the platform, paused to smile in amusement at the girl with the shiny brown hair and blue eyes.

Dan Aldrich steadied her as she slipped the shoe onto her slim foot. "Remember what I keep telling you about looking before you leap?" he asked, over the racket of other incoming and outgoing trains.

"I'm innocent," she grinned. "I didn't leap; I was pushed. I have thousands of witnesses." Kim sobered abruptly. She knew an agent's value often lay in his ability to go unnoticed. "Sorry about drawing attention to you."

They made their way up stairs and ramps to the so-called lower level of Grand Central, a place that was actually above the subway system. Here commuter trains disgorged passengers from the suburbs. Kim smiled impartially at them. Surprised, one or two nodded.

The Aldriches went on up marble stairs to the vast rotunda of the upper level. This was the point of arrival for visitors from far places. Cameras dangling from their shoulders, they gazed around in awe. Every morning Kim made a point of smiling warmly at the strangers. This was her city, and she wanted to make them feel welcome.

"Take it easy on this reception-committee-of-one bit," Dan said uneasily. "It's risky, Kim. Take that young man over there, the one who's ready to invite you for coffee because he thinks you gave him a come-on signal. He could be an armed killer.

"Or that perfectly innocent-looking grandmother type with the shopping bag stuffed with —what? Stolen securities? Dope? Think about it before you go rashly about, practically shaking hands."

Kim shivered. It was her father who rubbed shoulders with criminals. He was the one to worry about. Not Kim. Or so Kim believed.

Since he never discussed current cases, she had no way of knowing whether he was tracking a kidnapper or setting up a raid on a narcotics depot or looking for a cache of illegal weapons. He might be home tonight, or he might be in Puerto Rico or Canada or somewhere else. He might be able to phone a cryptic message in their special code that nobody else could understand—just in case an enemy were eavesdropping on the call. But he would be able to say only that he was going away, not where or for how long. She swung around to face him and ask him to be careful.

He was gone. He had simply vanished in the crowd. It was spooky.

A vague feeling of uneasiness swept over Kim. Envy, she chose to call it, rather than worry. Whichever, it went with her out the Lexington Avenue exit and toward the towering steel and glass building that housed WALCO Limited, World At Large Insurance Company.

She gazed up with pride. It might not be

Lloyds of London, but it was a close second, handling policies varied enough to defy the imagination, even an imagination as fertile as Kim's. And behind almost every policy was human drama. Insurance was not at all the impersonal field she had once believed. Perhaps the most important fact of all was the peace of mind that insurance provided to members of a harried, anxiety-ridden society.

"Security blanket," Kim said, laughing at the ludicrous comparison.

"I beg your pardon," said a startled old gentleman who had just come out of the enormous glass revolving door.

"I said 'security blanket,'" Kim repeated airily, as if that were the most natural remark in the world. Stifling a giggle, she whipped through the door, leaving the man to figure it out for himself—if he could.

In the elevator on the way up to the eighteenth floor, Kim amused herself by surreptitiously studying her fellow passengers. She often tried to figure out strangers, then make up lives for them and add families and friends. It was her nature to be curious, to wonder, to want to know.

That was one of the reasons she loved working at WALCO. It was company policy to have a new secretary rotate from department to department in order to gain an overall picture of operations. A girl was encouraged to study foreign languages and consider assignment in an overseas branch office after she had proved herself.

Right now Kim was serving as secretary to Mr. Rydell in the law department, eighteenth floor.

"Excuse me," she murmured as the car slid smoothly to a stop.

"Getting off!" snapped a tall, slightly paunchy man with gray hair, ignoring her completely and pushing his way out first. His attaché case banged into Kim's ribs.

She gave him a fair chance to be polite, then said sweetly, "I beg your pardon."

His cold, slate-colored eyes merely flicked over her before he turned on his heel. Cheeks blazing, Kim followed him down the hall. He marched through the doorway to Mr. Rydell's outer office, with Kim trotting along behind. The door swung back and caught her.

Okay, she thought. *I'll consign you to the mental category reserved for undesirables. The people who insure their wives and hope they'll die. The ones who put in false claims and try to defraud the insurance companies. The ones who dent a fender, then take a sledgehammer and make the car a total wreck so they can get a new one. You'd better watch out,* Kim thought darkly. *I'll keep my eye on you.*

He was standing at her desk, pounding a fist in exasperation. She made him wait while she went to the cloakroom and hung up her coat. Then, feeling a bit childish and sheepish, she asked what she could do for him.

"I want to see Mr. Rydell," he said. "Now."

"Do you have an appointment?"

"Young lady, whether or not I have an appointment is quite beside the point. Kindly tell Mr. Rydell I am here. Commissioner Saunders, of the town of Neadham."

Apparently Kim was supposed to be suitably awed. *Salaam, salaam, Excellency,* she thought, choking back a chortle. It wouldn't do to let the visitor, client or otherwise, think she was laughing at him. The object of humor was herself— as she might have been. Picture of Kim Aldrich keeping her cool, one shoe off and one shoe on, standing there like a lame duck. Blessings on the man who had pitched one alligator pump from the subway train.

"I'll see if Mr. Rydell is in," she said, her customary good humor restored. "I'll see if he can fit you into his schedule."

"He'll see me, all right." Mr. Saunders fumed. "If he isn't in, you can just find him and get him here on the double. We're insured with this company, and our town is being sued for five hundred thousand dollars."

Kim whistled, a shrill, through-the-teeth

screech (a hangover from a tomboy childhood),
spun around, and scooted to her boss's door.
Her sympathies were now with the visitor; no
wonder he was upset and rude. He could be
excused for the chip on his shoulder, at least
for the time being.

It was not yet nine o'clock, but luck was with
her. Mr. Rydell was in early.

"There's a Mr.—a Commissioner Saunders to
see you," she stuttered. "He's from Neadham.
That's a little town in Westchester County, on
Long Island Sound. I know, because we rented a
house in Rye, near Neadham, when I was little,
before my mother died—"

Oh, stop babbling, you idiot, she told herself.
But a half a million dollars! "He says the town
is being sued for five hundred thousand dollars!"

Mr. Rydell, a dark-haired man, graying a bit
at the temples, registered no emotion whatso-
ever. That was a lawyer for you, as Kim should
know, since her father had practiced law before
becoming an FBI agent.

"What kind of suit is it? Did he say?" asked
Mr. Rydell calmly. "Accident, negligence?"

Kim blushed. "I—I guess I forgot to ask."

"Be a good girl and find out, and bring me the
Neadham file. And show the commissioner in,
please."

It was an accident case. A seven-year-old boy

had fallen on the rocks that angled down the middle of the public beach at Neadham. On Labor Day, the last day the beach was officially open, he had sustained fractures of the skull and pelvis. It was now late October.

Kim placed the insurance file on Mr. Rydell's desk and waited, poised, to see if she was to remain in the room. She certainly hoped she could stay, because she wanted to know a lot of things about this case, especially how the little boy was getting along.

She remembered those rocks at Neadham vividly. She, her older brother Tom, who was now a copilot with Panoramic Airline, and her sister Cindy, now a nurse, had played there when they were youngsters. Kids naturally gravitated to the rocks to collect starfish and minnows and snails from the pools left in crevices when the tide went out. Kim had slipped and skinned her knee on the barnacles.

"Get your notebook, please, Miss Aldrich," said her boss. "I believe I'll have you take down Commissioner Saunders' verbal report."

Kim was back in a flash, seated beside the desk, pencil at the ready for shorthand.

"I want one thing understood from the beginning," said the commissioner. "There is to be no settlement. I didn't come crying to you to pay up, but merely to back our town up on a no-payment."

Mr. Rydell put his elbows on his desk and studied his hands, fingertips touching. "First we must get the facts straight, Commissioner," he said mildly. "However, there's an old rule of thumb: When a child is injured, the court usually makes an award—if the case comes to trial. It is often simpler to approach the plaintiff or his family and make a settlement to cover medical expenses. We are not in business to give money away, but, with a legitimate injury and claim—"

"There's another rule of thumb," interrupted Mr. Saunders, "that you can't fight City Hall. No, Mr. Rydell, there will be no settlement. We are not going to set a precedent and encourage everyone who uses public facilities to sue us."

"As insurers, Commissioner, we prefer to conduct an investigation, make our own determination as to the legitimacy of the claim—"

"Hah! You can save your time and take my word for it. The claim is false," snapped Saunders. "We will go to trial, and we'll win hands down. We can prove contributory negligence on the part of the child and his mother. They had absolutely no right to be on the rocks. The area was roped off and clearly marked, 'Keep Off.' "

"Oh, but—" Kim protested, then bit her tongue. Her boss signaled for her to continue.

"The rocks used to be open to the public. Maybe it's not true anymore, but they used to spray the rocks with some kind of chemical every two or three days to remove the slippery algae. Then it was okay for the kids to play there. I mean, maybe they'd risk a scratch or something—but that's par for the course, no matter where kids play. I know it was legal for kids, because they stationed a lifeguard right there on the rocks."

"Well, Commissioner?" Mr. Rydell probed.

"When I say the child was off limits, I mean just that, whether or not your secretary believes me," snapped Saunders, flicking a cold glance at Kim. "I can assure her that the rock area is clearly marked. The boy was trespassing, and we would be justified to prosecute him. Perhaps we will do precisely that—prosecute."

He opened his attaché case and extracted a snapshot of the beach, the rocks, and the pier at Neadham. Kim recognized it, even though the "Keep Off" signs and the ropes were new to her. She frowned and bent to get a closer look.

"You see?" said Saunders triumphantly. "Contributory negligence. Trespassing. There will be no settlement."

Kim kept staring at the picture. The signs and the ropes looked new. *New*—that was the clue. Long Island Sound is a saltwater body. Salt water quickly weathers painted signs and ropes. The signs and ropes were new, and that wasn't the only peculiar thing about the picture.

"Questions, Miss Aldrich?" prompted Mr. Rydell.

"We don't need questions or opinions from a two-bit stenographer," snorted Saunders.

"Secretary," corrected Mr. Rydell imperturbably. "As for questions and opinions, we encourage all our staff to ask, to think, to become involved in company business. And we promote from within the ranks. Miss Aldrich, for example, has a feeling for this field. Perhaps one day she will become an investigator."

Miss Aldrich, meanwhile, was on the spot. If she spoke up, Mr. Saunders would be annoyed, and a client's feathers mustn't be ruffled by a minor employee. That was Rule One at Miss Axminster's school of secretarial skills. On the other hand, if Miss Aldrich backed down, her boss would think she did not have a feel for insurance, after all. Okay, but the real point was that WALCO was the insurer, and there was something odd here.

"If the picture were taken during the summer, when the accident occurred, the ropes and signs would be weathered. Right? But this picture was taken after the summer. See? In summer there would be a lot of people around, people in swimsuits."

"Nonsense!" Saunders snapped. "Pictures can be taken at night, after the people have left. With lights. A strobe light."

"Yes, but it wasn't taken during the summer," Kim persisted. "There's a man at the end of the pier. He's a little blurry, but I'm sure he's wearing a heavy jacket. Of course," she backtracked quickly, "the picture could have been taken before the summer season began."

If it had been taken in early spring, showing the beach as it was prepared for the summer season, it would indeed prove that the boy was at fault. But if it had been taken after the beach closed, after the accident, something else might be proved. Something ugly, like signs and ropes put up after the fact, to disprove a legitimate claim.

2
strictly
routine

Normally Kim slept like a top, but tonight she was spooked because her father, brother, and sister were, for once, all away from home at the same time. In addition, she had a weird feeling of foreboding about her job. She dozed fitfully, beset by snatches of worrisome dreams.

There was a vivid replay of her father's phone call just before she left her office. "I'm calling from a phone booth, so I can't talk long," he had said.

It was a family code. It meant someone might be trying to listen in on the conversation. It meant Kim must ask no questions, because an agent following a criminal might himself be under surveillance. The code meant that Dan Aldrich was going away, and no one must ask where or for how long.

"Strictly routine," Dan had said to reassure his daughter. He always said that, no matter how dangerous his current case.

And there was a snatch of dream about Kim's brother leaving for a flight to Houston, Texas. "Strictly routine," said Tom. But he might be hijacked and wind up in Cuba—or decide to put up a fight.

And the wire from Cindy saying she had been called up for disaster duty with the Red Cross. "Routine flood duty in Maine, so don't worry."

Ha! Don't worry, they said. It was okay when they said it individually, but this time they all said it at once. *And me with a weekend coming up, and nothing to do but worry,* fretted Kim, punching her pillow.

"All right," she said aloud, "I'll put my mind to work on my own business: the Neadham case."

Fact: A seven-year-old boy had been injured on Labor Day.

Fact: The town of Neadham was being sued for a half million dollars.

Why such an enormous sum? Why not a reasonable amount, enough to cover medical expenses?

Question: Were the boy's parents mere opportunists, as Commissioner Saunders claimed? Or, as he had further insinuated, had they deliberately encouraged the child to go to a dangerous place?

"No!" Kim had protested, aghast. "I don't believe it."

"People will do many things for money," Saunders had said cynically, "especially if they're in debt."

Question: *Were* the Maddens—the boy's name was Peter Madden—in debt? Was reckless installment buying their trouble? Were they behind in mortgage payments and in danger of losing their home—or was this merely a diabolical doubt planted by Saunders to discredit the Maddens?

Question: How was the boy, Pete? Didn't anybody care whether or not he was suffering? Would he ever get well, be able to run, swim, play in the Little League, skate?

"He's malingering," Mr. Saunders had snorted. "He is out of the hospital. Mark my words, he has been well coached to pretend he can't walk, to pretend he has headaches, to pretend he has tingling in his hands."

Question: Why was Commissioner Saunders so insistent that there must be no settlement?

Fact: The town of Neadham was insured for only one hundred thousand dollars for a single accident case. That meant an additional four hundred thousand dollars for which the town could be liable if it lost its case in court.

Presumption: A settlement could be made within the insured amount, provided an offer were made before going to trial.

Question: Was it not more logical to try for a settlement, rather than to risk a court verdict? Why was Mr. Saunders so positive the plaintiff would lose his case? Doesn't the jury usually sympathize with a child? Isn't that basic psychology?

Question: Was the picture rigged? If so, might there not be other rigged evidence? Or was the entire matter of skulduggery a figment of Kim Aldrich's fertile imagination?

"The facts will come to light during our investigation," Mr. Rydell had said.

"Routine investigation, no doubt!" Kim snorted aloud in her darkened room. Okay, granted that much of the world's work is routine, and granted that routine research is necessary, even interesting. But Saturday was coming up, and there was no way to get on with things until Monday.

Kim doted on suspense stories, but she always read the end of the book first—just so she'd be sure everything came out all right. If only she could read the end of the Neadham case. Frustrating.

Fact: There wasn't a thing she could do about it until Monday. Even then she'd be on the sidelines, waiting, asking questions, wishing she were the investigator.

Solution: Find something else to keep her busy, mentally and physically.

Kim was up and dressed by seven o'clock. She ran a comb through her shining brown hair and gave thanks for the slight curl nature had bestowed upon her. Imagine having to sleep in rollers!

She made a face at herself in the mirror. Aside from a faint shadowing under the eyes, she didn't look too bad, considering her fitful sleep. The yellow turtleneck sweater and camel's hair slacks looked okay.

"Morning, Gerta," she said, wandering out to the kitchen in search of nourishment.

The plump housekeeper, who had cared for the Aldriches since Kim's mother had died, smiled dotingly. "You sit right down, and I'll fix you some orange juice, bacon, eggs, coffee. And how about some nice popovers?"

"Um, breakfast's my favorite meal, but what are you trying to do to me? Gerta, I think I'll have to move away and go on a diet."

Gerta reached out and gave her an affectionate whack. "You need some meat on your bones. Look at you; no more than a hundred ten pounds soaking wet. Now eat and listen to me. Someday, when you grow up, you will want a man to fall in love with you and marry you. Men like women who are—"

"I'm grown up now," teased Kim.

"Pooh, you're still a baby."

Being the youngest had its drawbacks. Kim's father, her brother, her sister, and Gerta—especially Gerta—tended to treat her like a child. She fought against it, but, so far, she hadn't accomplished anything important enough to win full adult status.

"I think I'll take a flying lesson," she announced.

Gerta reacted with predictable shock. "You'll be the death of us or of yourself. Flying lessons, humph! It was bad enough when you were falling out of trees. Then you persuaded your father to get you that fast little sports car. And last year you decided to take up sky diving. Broke your arm, too, didn't you? Flying!"

It was a token objection. She hadn't gone into even half of Kim's pursuits of challenge. If she had really meant it, she would have at least brought up the time Kim had managed to foul up her breathing hose when she went skin diving. And the time she'd been conked on the head by a surfboard.

"Want to come with me?" asked Kim.

Now the shock was genuine. "You'd never get me up in one of those machines! It's not natural. People were supposed to stay on the ground. Next thing, you'll be trying to be the girl astronaut, first girl to go to the moon. Me, I stay where I belong."

"See you later, then. I'll be home for dinner. Thanks for the yummy breakfast."

"You be careful."

"Flying is just routine. Ask Tom. Sure you don't want to come?" Kim ducked a well-aimed

dishcloth, picked up her jacket, and headed out
to the elevator.

Down on the lower level of the building, she
slid behind the wheel of her pride and joy, a
sleek little red Triumph. She pushed the gadget
on the dash, raising the garage doors by remote
control, revved up, and drove out.

She eased her way over to Franklin Delano
Roosevelt Drive, parallel to the East River, and
headed north—to the Triboro Bridge, to the
Bruckner Expressway, to the Cross Bronx Expressway, to the New England Thruway. She
told herself she was going directly to the Westchester County Airport.

She kept telling herself that for a half hour,
then admitted she just might have been kidding
herself from the start. This was certainly not
the shortest route to the airport—not to mention
the fact that she should have made an appointment in advance if she expected to find an in-
structor available.

There, at her right, was the exit sign for
Neadham. She made the turn, threaded her way
through the treelined streets ablaze with autumn colors, then on to the shore and to the
beach.

As long as she was here, by accident or de-
sign, she might as well get out and look around.
Not that she'd learn anything about the Maddens, but just to look. She parked the Triumph,

pocketed the keys, and followed the path to the entrance gate. The turnstile she remembered vaguely from her childhood was gone. Probably stored for the winter.

She went down steep steps to a concrete deck, and on past the stone building that housed a lunch counter, First Aid headquarters, lockers, and showers. Now she was facing the sparkling blue Sound.

It was a clear, beautiful day. Sometimes, she remembered, Long Island seemed a million miles away. Today, on the opposite shore, it seemed almost within touching distance—but your arm would have to be five miles long!

The rock area, where Pete Madden had fallen, was directly ahead, sloping down to the water. On Kim's right was a crescent of sand. The pier was at her left, blocking a view of another spit of sand. She had the uneasy feeling that Commissioner Saunders might round the corner of the building at any minute. Guilty conscience for being here and snooping?

Well, what of it? She had a perfect right to be here, didn't she? Commissioner Saunders was a client of her company, and he should be glad to know she was interested enough in the Neadham case to come.

Only he wouldn't be pleased at all. Mr. Saunders, she knew, would only accuse her of meddling. He was already annoyed at her for poking a few holes in his story. No indeed; Commissioner Saunders would not at all approve of her presence. And Kim Aldrich had no desire to see him. It would ruin her day. But Kim knew someone was behind her, watching her. Commissioner Saunders? Well, she would just face him and get it over.

She swung around to meet him—and found herself looking into the brown eyes of a total stranger.

He was about six feet tall, broad shouldered and rangy, his face still bearing traces of what must have been a deep summer tan. He might have been a lifeguard—or a sailor, one of the group who sailed practically all year on the Sound. Maybe he even crewed on the Bermuda races.

And there I go again, Kim thought, *making up a whole life story for him on the basis of one glimpse. But he is attractive. Mighty attractive.*

"Hi," he said with a friendly grin.

Kim looked around to make sure there was no Commissioner Saunders or anyone else. She grinned back. Camera in hand, he approached.

Well, she'd done it again—encouraged a stranger. Maybe he had narcotics concealed in the camera, she thought. Not really, of course, not this young man, surely not one who was so interesting and friendly. *Quiet, Dad. This one's okay.*

"Excuse me, but I wonder if you'd pose for me right over there, with the rocks just behind you," he said.

"Why?"

"Good question." He paused, studied her reflectively, and suggested tentatively, "I could say it's because I enjoy taking pictures of pretty girls. As a matter of fact, I do enjoy it, or would if I ever had time. Would you buy that reason?"

Kim shook her head. He'd already practically admitted he had a definite reason not associated with pleasure. Besides, maybe it wasn't a great idea to have a stranger in possession of pictures of her—not without a very good reason.

"Why?" she demanded stubbornly.

"Well, all right." He had reached a decision. "I'm working on a legal case. Kid was injured on those rocks. I need a picture taken after the accident to prove that certain things have changed since the day the boy was hurt."

"Who are you?" Kim demanded.

"Name's Andy Hill. I'm a lawyer."

For the plaintiff, Kim figured. He must be, if he wanted to prove "certain changes." Such as new ropes and signs?

"What good is a picture?" she asked. "I can see that you can prove it's not summer now, because there are no boats moored in the harbor and because I'm wearing warm clothes. But you could have taken such a picture before the accident—even last spring. What can you prove?"

"I can dig up a snapshot taken the day of the accident, if I'm lucky," he answered. "Surely, with the crowd that was here on Labor Day, someone must have taken some snapshots. As for today's picture, you'll be my proof. I could always subpoena you as a witness," he added lightly, teasing.

Not teasing at all, Kim figured. He'd find her, too, by tracing the license number on her car or something.

"Why me?" she persisted. "Why didn't you get some friend of yours—"

"I'd rather have a disinterested stranger testify about the date of this picture. It would impress the jury more favorably." He grabbed her arm and said hurriedly, "Here comes the enemy. Don't mention this picture idea. It would only alert Commissioner Saunders and, for all I know, any available Labor Day snapshots might vanish before I could see them."

Commissioner Saunders. "The enemy," Andy had called him. And Kim, too, was the enemy in a sense, only Andy didn't know it. Pity.

Saunders bore down on them, fire in his eyes.

"What are you doing here?" he demanded.

"Sir?" the lawyer said.

"Not you," snorted the commissioner. "I can guess you're here trying to build a case on thin air. I mean her." He stabbed a finger at Kim.

"What kind of collusion is going on around here? What is the secretary of the legal officer of our insurance company doing comparing notes with the attorney for the opposition?"

Andy's jaw dropped. "A spy?"

"A traitor," charged Saunders.

"I never saw him before in my life," gasped Kim, "and that's the truth."

She turned and fled from two pairs of accusing eyes—and slipped on a rock. She clawed at the air and knew, sickeningly, that she was going to slide right under the rope and crash on the rocks below.

3
miss
fixit

Two pairs of hands reached out to Kim. For a split second of madness, it seemed that they were trying to push her over the cliff.

Money, she thought wildly. Saunders had said a person would do almost anything for money. Andy Hill thought she was a spy trying to wreck his case. He stood to earn a fat fee if he won a half-million-dollar settlement for his client. Maybe he was an opportunist eliminating a threat.

Saunders—she hadn't trusted him from the start. There had to be a reason why he was so violently opposed to her questioning of the case. Maybe he was hiding something.

In either event, murder could be committed easily right now. One man could push her and the other would believe the push was a fumbled attempt to save her.

And then, miraculously, she was safe in Andy's arms. It was like dying and going to heaven.

"I love you," she wanted to burst out, clinging to him until her legs stopped trembling. Instead, she grinned weakly and said, "Whew, I almost fell for you then, didn't I?" It was against her principles to admit that Kim Aldrich was capable of hitting the panic button.

If Andy Hill held her a bit longer than necessary, was it because he, too, had had a sudden special feeling? Wishful thinking on her part? Possibly. *Probably,* she decided reluctantly. And yet—and yet there was a magic instant when time seemed to stand still, when they seemed to be the only people in the world.

Commissioner Saunders ruined it. "I suggest you go back where you belong and stop meddling!" he snapped.

Andy snapped right back. "And I suggest she's in no condition to drive at the moment!" He set Kim down on her feet but kept a protective arm on her shoulder. "Buy you a cup of coffee?"

It seemed like a lovely idea, in spite of Dan Aldrich's warnings about strange young men making exactly such offers. Kim was about to nod.

"As long as she is in this town, I'll just go right along with Miss Fixit, too," Saunders announced. "If there's to be any conversation between the opposition and our attorney's staff, I'm going to be right there."

The prospect of Commissioner Saunders' company was anything but attractive. "I'm all right," Kim said. "I was really on my way to the airport to see if I could take a flying lesson. I just stopped off here on a whim." *An almost fatal whim,* she thought. "I guess I'll get going."

There! She had dropped a perfectly good clue. If Andy, too, had felt that flash of magic, he could easily throw Saunders off the track and follow her. That would enable her to avoid antagonizing a client, and, after all, he *was* a client. She must never forget it. But she and Andy could have that coffee, after all—and go on from there—maybe.

Both men walked toward the parking lot with her. Her little TR looked like a midget beside a sleek, black Cadillac. Air-conditioned, no doubt, Kim figured. Nothing but the best for Commissioner Saunders. It had to be his car, because it hadn't been there when she pulled in, and Andy had arrived ahead of her.

Question: What salary does a commissioner draw? Does a small town like Neadham provide Cadillacs?

"Can I give you a lift?" Kim asked Andy. *No, Commissioner, I didn't offer merely to needle you,* she added silently. *It was merely a spontaneous gesture of courtesy. Mostly.*

"No, thanks," Andy answered. "Victoria's waiting for me."

Kim's heart did a flip. She should have known there would be a girl somewhere. Any man as attractive as Andy would surely have a girl— or a wife.

"Then don't keep her waiting any longer," Kim suggested lightly, suddenly very busy trying to locate her car keys in her slacks pockets.

"Hey, would you like to meet Victoria? She's pretty special, if I do say so myself," Andy said enthusiastically. "She's over there, on the far side of the building. Come on."

Kim couldn't think of a single reason why she would want to meet Andy Hill's girl, or how she could avoid it without broadcasting her precipitate interest in Andy. She went with him. So did Commissioner Saunders.

There was no one there. The only thing in sight was a venerable Model A car. It was painted a deep green and shone as if it had just come from the showroom. It was an antique of beauty, and Kim fell for it. It was an old-time vehicle with real character.

"Doesn't she remind you of a dowager?" Andy grinned, patting the hood affectionately. "Of course, she's really not as old as the queen, but somehow the name suits her."

She was indeed special, and so was the man who owned her, Kim decided promptly. At her urging, Andy gave her a quick history. He had bought a wreck, restored it completely, and now belonged to an antique car club.

"We go to rallies, sort of like you sports car

nuts," Andy explained, "only we have a modern station wagon as escort, filled with spare parts in case of breakdowns. Actually, Victoria runs like a dream because I rebuilt the engine from scratch. I could probably give your little red bug a run for its money."

Kim was dying to take him up on the challenge. Unfortunately, the WALCO client was still there, and, no matter what temptation, she hadn't better incur any further disapproval. She had to let the matter drop.

There was nothing for it but to leave, go to the airport, and wait, hoping for the best. When and if Andy showed up, she'd ask him to let her drive Victoria. Love me, love my car; that would be Andy.

The only trouble was that Andy didn't show up at the airport. Kim waited at Westair, the flying school, for over an hour. Then she drove around the field to the tower side and waited again, in the restaurant. She waited outside.

Drat! There were *two* airports in Westchester County. The other one, a small field without a control tower, was in Armonk. There was a flying school in Armonk, too. Maybe he'd gone there, and he wouldn't be able to trace her, because he didn't even know her name.

Pipe dream. The whole idea was a nothing. If he had had the slightest intention of seeing her again, he'd have asked her name in the first place. *And so much for that brainstorm, Kim Aldrich,* she told herself ruefully.

She would have put the entire meeting out of her mind except for one thing: She felt that she should report it to Mr. Rydell on Monday. She was afraid he'd be annoyed at her meddling, but still she had to tell him.

Happily, he heard her out without apparent disapproval. "As a matter of fact, I'm having lunch with Mr. Hill today," he said.

That was an odd turn of events, if ever Kim had met one. Surely Mr. Rydell wasn't himself involved in some sort of devious plot-counter-plot! No, of course not. Opposing lawyers often met and discussed cases without revealing privileged information. She should have remembered that from her father's days as a practicing trial attorney. And yet. . . .

"Would you like to join us for lunch, Miss Aldrich?" asked Mr. Rydell. "It will be a working meeting. I may need you to take notes."

Kim's heart leaped. Now she could admit to herself she had been considering all sorts of ways to meet Andy Hill again. She had even thought of trading her TR for a Model A—if worst came to worst—and joining his club.

"Yes, of course, Mr. Rydell," she said as casually as possible.

The rest of the morning dragged. Fortunately, her current work consisted mostly of routine reports to be typed. She had trouble keeping her mind on business.

Andy Hill's face kept popping up between her and the typewriter. Every detail was clear. Brown eyes that held a glint of humor. Right eyebrow that quirked when he grinned. Dark hair cut short, as befitted a legal eagle, but that didn't mean he lacked the confidence needed for originality; witness Victoria. Slight cleft in the strong chin. Hint of a bump in an otherwise perfectly chiseled nose. Football injury?

Married? Engaged? Ah, well, at least Kim was wearing blue today. Much as she adored yellow, blue did glamorous things to her eyes, turning them almost gentian. She was almost tempted to dash out during her coffee break and invest in a set of false eyelashes. On second thought, no. Ten to one she'd drop one in her soup.

One way or another, Kim survived until noon. Mr. Rydell had said one o'clock. She was ready at five to, hair combed, lipstick freshened, cheeks vivid from excitement. Little white gloves, a dab of white lilac perfume behind each ear, a wisp of blue veil atop her head in lieu of a hat. She rapped softly on Mr. Rydell's door. Adventure-prone? She certainly felt like it.

They rode down to Fourteenth Street in a cab.

They were to meet Andy Hill at Luchow's, one of Kim's favorite restaurants. Luchow's had an air of elegance, with its beamed ceilings, snowy tablecloths, and old-world courteous service. Even the bartenders—German, Austrian, and Swiss—fit right into the atmosphere while they served German, Austrian, Swiss, Danish, or Swedish beer in enormous steins imported along with the beer.

Other places might go modern with glass walls and psychedelic lighting, but Luchow's remained true to its heritage. It had long been a favorite of New York's elite. Such legendary figures as Diamond Jim Brady and Lillian Russell had been devotees of the place, remembered here for their fabulous after-the-theater suppers.

Yes, Luchow's had a charm all its own. Kim liked it even better today because a rangy, weather-beaten young man was there, rising to greet them. His eyes lighted in appreciation when the girl extended her hand to him.

"Yes, of course, you two have met," murmured Mr. Rydell.

"How's Victoria?" Kim asked.

"Very well, thank you. She sends her regards." Andy's face was quite solemn; only his right eyebrow quirked.

"You didn't bring her?"

"No. She's not particularly fond of the city." Mr. Rydell looked heavenward in thanksgiving. This was to be a working luncheon, and he obviously felt that Victoria, whoever she might be, would be surplus company.

Kim slanted a quick glance at Andy, just to verify the fact that they were on the same wavelength, then looked away. It would be most unpolitic if the two of them erupted into laughter.

When they were seated, Mr. Rydell sidestepped further delay by suggesting that they all have sauerbraten, potato dumplings, and tossed salad, specialties of the house.

"Now then," Mr. Rydell said, when the meal had been successfully launched, "let's get down to cases."

"Fire away, Counselor," said Andy amiably.

"First, if—repeat, *if*—we are willing to offer a reasonable settlement, would your clients consider such an offer?"

"Counselor, you're asking me to commit my clients before the fact." Andy grinned.

Touché, applauded Kim silently.

Mr. Rydell bowed slightly. "We request permission for our company physician to examine the boy. Such an examination would be necessary before we could possibly offer a settlement."

"Fair enough. Anything else?"

"Yes, I'd like to talk to the boy and his mother myself. And I'd like Miss Aldrich to be there to take notes."

He'll never agree to that, Kim thought.

"I see nothing wrong with that," Andy said, surprisingly. "However," he added, "I would naturally have to be present at such a meeting, to instruct my clients on their answers to your questions."

"Off the record, Andy," Mr. Rydell said, dropping his formal manner, "you will advise your clients to accept a reasonable settlement to cover medical expenses, won't you?"

"Not on your life," Andy replied firmly.

"You're a smart young fellow, Andy. You can go far in this profession if you'll just be realistic. You made your first mistake by asking too much money. A half a million! Be reasonable. You'd be well advised to accept a settlement to cover medical expenses. If you insist on going to trial, the jury, consciously or subconsciously, will be unfavorably impressed by your clients' obvious greed—or their attorney's," Mr. Rydell added softly.

The barb drew blood; Andy's face flamed. Yes, Kim thought, if he settled for medical expenses, his fee would be minimal, probably less than a hundred dollars. A pittance. But if he won a court case, he could earn as much as fifty thousand. Quite a difference; perhaps well worth the gamble.

"I should ignore that," Andy said, "but I'm not going to. I'm going to trial because of principle. There's more here than money, more even than an injured boy."

"You're taking a real risk, Counselor, if I read your meaning correctly. You're risking your professional career; perhaps a good deal more than that."

"What good is a career in law—or even my physical safety—if I don't demand justice?" Andy retorted.

So he was either an opportunist or a crusader. Kim didn't know exactly what he meant by the allusion to personal safety, but intuition told her he was facing a very real danger—or else she was dreaming up an adventure out of whole cloth.

4
a case
of fraud?

The sensible thing to do, Kim decided on her
way back to the office with Mr. Rydell, was to
put Andy Hill out of her mind. Yes, but knowing
what was sensible and *being* sensible were two
different things; worrying about him was more
in character.

Anyway, circumstances conspired to keep
Andy in the forefront of her mind. She was
closely involved with the Neadham file, which
grew steadily. There were copies of X rays of
the Madden boy's injuries. Statements from
various Neadham officials had to be taken down
in shorthand and then transcribed. Pictures and
reports submitted by Chris Townsend, the
WALCO investigator, had to be studied.

And Andy Hill, naturally, was working on the
opposite side of the case. He was there, in the
flesh, when Mr. Rydell, the WALCO physician,
and Kim arrived in Neadham for their Thursday interview with the plaintiffs.

The Madden home was a little cracker box of
a house with artificial brick siding. It was located on a shabby street at the outskirts of town.

Andy met the WALCO contingent at the door and introduced them to the mother of the injured boy.

Mrs. Madden was a tall, thin woman with dark eyes and black hair that was graying. She might well have been a beauty when she was young, with her delicate bone structure. It was difficult to guess her age because she looked so harried, but she appeared to be mid-fortyish, Kim thought.

"My husband couldn't afford to take the day off," she said, twisting her hands nervously. "Mr. Hill said it was all right, though, because he wasn't with us when Pete got hurt. I was there. I saw it all." Her eyes clouded with the memory.

Kim spotted a child-sized wheelchair.

"Pete's in bed," said his mother. "He doesn't feel well."

The visitors made appropriate murmurs of sympathy, then got down to the business at hand: Mrs. Madden's version of the accident.

"He was playing on the rocks like always. All the little boys play—played—there. He stood up to wave to me, and, just like that, he went flying right over the other children's heads. He landed flat on his back. I thought he was dead." She covered her face with her hands.

The rest of the story came out in bits and pieces. Crowds of adults rushing to the boy, frantically insistent on moving him to higher ground, to the pier, anywhere, just to be moving him. A lifeguard warning them to leave the boy alone, not to touch him. Police sirens. White-coated attendants with a stretcher. An ambulance.

"I thought he was dead," repeated Mrs. Madden. "I—all the way to the hospital he didn't move. He was in the operating room for hours." She wept into a handkerchief.

Her attorney placed a comforting hand on her shoulder and turned to the visitors, his eyes blazing. In a controlled voice he announced, "I think my client has been through enough."

"If we might talk to the boy . . ." Mr. Rydell prompted softly.

Mrs. Madden pulled herself together and led the way to a back bedroom. Kim, directly behind her, felt rather than actually saw a flurry of activity. Unless she missed her guess, Pete Madden had been out of bed or, at the very least, down at the foot of his bed, trying to tune in to the conversation about him and his accident.

Why, the little scamp, Kim thought, grinning to herself. *That little fraud!* Abruptly, she stopped smiling, because fraud might be a very real aspect of this case.

Whatever the possibility of motion, Pete was lying perfectly still when the group entered his room. He looked like a bona fide invalid, and surely there was no way he could have faked his pallor. His vast crop of freckles stood out starkly on his pale face.

Kim's heart went out to him. He was a stocky little boy with carrot-red hair, vivid blue eyes, and a snub nose. A boy like this shouldn't be confined to bed or a wheelchair, she thought, stricken. This was a rugged little guy who should be out swinging by his knees from the branch of a tree, playing football, skating, riding a bike.

His account of the accident was blunt. "I went flying. I thought I was going to heaven for sure. I didn't wake up for three days, and then they—and then they told me I'd never be a big league ballplayer. They said I wouldn't even play Little League."

"They're going to pay," Mrs. Madden said furiously. "They're going to pay through the nose. They *did* this to my son! It's their fault, and—"

"Easy," murmured Andy, his hand again on her shoulder. "Let me do the talking, in and out of court, hm?"

Money, thought Kim. But all the money in the world wouldn't make things up to a boy like this. He'd lose more than the ability to walk, too, unless she read the mother wrong. He'd lose a sunny, happy-go-lucky nature and he'd become bitter after a while, when hope was gone.

"Son, it's foolish to decide everything is hopeless," the insurance doctor said. "Give yourself time to get well. Do the exercises your surgeon has told you to do. Keep trying, and—"

"Huh, a lot you know about it. Who are you, anyway?" Pete demanded.

"As a matter of fact, I know quite a bit about broken bones. I'm a doctor myself."

"Get away from me!" Pete said shrilly, hiding under the bedclothes.

"The doctor just wants to examine you," Mr. Rydell explained.

"No." Pete's voice was muffled but determined.

"Come on, Champ," Andy Hill urged. "I told you—"

"Please, Pete," begged the boy's mother.

"No!"

It looked like a stalemate.

"My brother is a pilot," Kim said suddenly. "I take flying lessons."

A cautious eye peered out from beneath the covers. Then Pete let out a wail. "That's a dirty trick, rubbing it in. I can't even walk, and I'll never be able to fly or—or—or anything."

"Pooh," said Kim. "There was a famous pilot in World War Two, an Englishman, who lost both his legs and learned to fly again. And one of our Navy fliers lost one leg and was discharged from service. It took him two years, but he proved he could still fly, and the Navy took him back."

She had his attention and he wanted to hear more, but he still wanted no part of doctors. He needed more shock treatment. "Stop feeling so sorry for yourself," she said cruelly, because sometimes cruelty is the only true kindness. "Let's get the show on the road. Let the doctor look you over. *Anything* is better than just lying there doing nothing, Pete."

"Will you take me up in a plane if I do?"

"That's bribery." Kim laughed. She knew she had won that round, but she had to be fair and honest. "I'm not allowed to take passengers up yet, because I only have a student pilot's license."

"Huh, I might have known." Pete burrowed under the bedding again.

"I'll make a bargain with you," she announced. "I'll race you. You do your exercises and hurry up and get strong enough to go up in a plane. I'll hurry up and earn my regular license. If I beat you, I'll wait to take you up. If you beat me, I'll get my brother to take you. He's an honest-to-goodness commercial pilot. He's—"

She bit off the rest. It would, indeed, be rubbing it in to tell how Tom Aldrich had flown a scout plane in Vietnam, how he had won the Distinguished Flying Cross.

"Promise?" Pete demanded.

"Promise. Cross my heart. Shake?"

A hand crept out from the sheets and gripped hers.

"You have no right to get his hopes up like that," Mrs. Madden burst out. "He's sick. He can't expect—he'll never—"

Oh, darn. Oh, darn, darn, darn! Kim raged inwardly. *What's the matter with the woman? The boy has to have something to look forward to. He has to have some hope! She's his mother; surely she must know. Even if he could never walk, he could get well enough to go up in a plane, even on a stretcher.*

"Opportunist," Commissioner Saunders had labeled her. The accusation had appalled Kim because she simply couldn't accept a mother who would use her child for monetary gain. Now, sick inside, she wondered if the charge were true.

Meanwhile, there was the boy, a real human being. A boy who had sustained painful and serious injuries that might or might not be permanent. The mental injuries his mother was subjecting him to could be more serious than the fractures.

To be reasonably just, Kim admitted to herself, she had to acknowledge the fact that Mrs. Madden could be merely an overly protective mother. That, too, was destructive. But Kim

Aldrich really had no business overriding the mother—and no business abandoning the child, depending on which way you looked at things.

"Let the doctor examine you, okay?" she said gently. "As for flying, Pete, I'll keep tabs on you. As soon as you're strong, we'll ask your own doctor about it. If he tells your mom it's all right—" She flicked a glance at Mrs. Madden.

The physician stepped into the breach. "Fine. Now, suppose everyone step outside while I examine the patient."

"You stay," Pete ordered Kim.

"Then I'll stay," Andy announced.

"I'm staying," Mrs. Madden put in flatly. "I don't want her filling his head with nonsense, getting up false hopes. Flying, hmph!"

The doctor shooed them all out. They waited in the living room—and heard a piercing scream.

"That hurts," cried Pete. "Ow, ow, you hurt!"

Mrs. Madden leaped to her feet, then sat down abruptly, her hands clenched. "They're going to pay," she muttered. "The insurance company is going to pay. The town is going to pay."

Kim battled her own instinct to rush to the boy, won the fight, and studied the mother. Was she acting? Had she coached Pete to pretend greater pain than he really felt? After all, the doctor knew what he was doing; he surely wasn't torturing the child.

She wished she knew more about this family, knew what made them tick.

The doctor rejoined them shortly. He was noncommittal. "I believe that's all we need. Thank you, Mrs. Madden. You can go back in now. And, Miss Aldrich, the boy asked that you go back to say good-bye."

"May I?" she asked the mother.

"I guess it's all right," the woman answered grudgingly.

Kim would have liked to stay awhile with Pete, just to give him things to think about outside the sickroom. It seemed a better tactical move to make it a quick farewell, in the hope that she could keep in touch with the boy.

"Don't forget, you promised," Pete said.

"I won't forget," she answered, resisting the urge to bend down and kiss the tip of his freckled nose, a move that might have offended his manly dignity. She shook his hand instead and rejoined the others in the living room.

Mr. Rydell glanced at his watch and decided it was too late to go back to the office. Instead, he said, he would go upcounty to see another client, as long as he was so close. The doctor might as well accompany him.

Kim had a distinct hunch that the two men were seizing the opportunity to play a round of golf, especially since her boss suggested she return to the city by train.

"I'll drop you at the station," Mr. Rydell said. "Take the rest of the afternoon off."

"I'll take her to the station, sir," Andy offered, "if you have no objection to your secretary consorting with the opposition."

Mr. Rydell took exception to the term. They were not, he stated dryly, opponents. They were both on the side of justice. Furthermore, Miss Aldrich would be unable to divulge any trial strategy, even if she were the type to do so. Reason: She would have no access to such information, because her boss was not going to defend the suit against the town of Neadham.

It had come as a disappointment to Kim to discover that the WALCO law department conducted its own investigation but did not defend suit. A WALCO attorney would attend the trial and offer what assistance he could, but he would remain in the background. Ordinarily, a regular town attorney would defend.

"Not in this case, however," Mr. Rydell went on. "There is a large sum of money involved, too large for the regular man. No, the city fathers have called in Duncan MacKenzie, no less. A nationally famous trial lawyer. Brilliant."

Andy whistled. "Looks as if I'll be playing in the big league."

"Don't say I didn't warn you," the older man said. "It's your neck. Speaking of warnings"— Mr. Rydell smiled slightly—"ten to one Miss

Aldrich will pick your brains. She has the makings of an insurance investigator. She'll get more out of you than you realize. Just a friendly tip."

"I'll watch myself." Andy grinned.

"See that you do." Mr. Rydell was no longer smiling. "See that you take good care of my secretary. She is not expendable."

Andy nodded, took Kim's elbow, and steered her to the door. "Come along; Victoria's waiting." When he had her ensconced in his venerable conveyance, he suggested, "Let's get that coffee we almost had. You don't really want to get on a train just yet, do you?"

She certainly did not. This was a golden opportunity to do some sleuthing, and Mr. Rydell had given tacit approval—well, hadn't he? She wanted to talk, find out everything Andy knew about the Maddens. And she wanted to find out about Andy himself, make up her mind about his motives, dig deeper into this recurrent allusion to professional and physical danger.

But first things first. Her father had taught her the basics of research. The local newspaper was a good starting point, for its morgue might contain a file on the person under investigation. News stories, wedding stories, birth announcements, pictures, all sorts of bits and scraps could add up to a sizable fund of background information.

Her dad also contacted power companies, telephone companies, banks, stores, neighbors, to find out the habits of his subjects. Those particular sources were closed to Kim because she lacked the proper credentials to gain entrée and examine confidential records.

Newspapers, however, required no such credentials. The reason was obvious: Once a story was published, it was no longer confidential.

"Well, where would you like to go?" Andy prompted.

"To the local paper, before they close for the day."

Andy stared at her; then he began to laugh. "Your boss wasn't just kidding, was he? You really go after information like a dog after a bone. If you ever want to switch jobs, let me know. If I win this case, I'll be a partner in my firm, and I'll sign you on as my combination secretary-legman."

So. Andy Hill had a lot more to gain than money; he had the chance of a partnership. How come, though, that a junior member of his firm had been assigned to such an important case? "Do you think you'll win?" Kim couldn't resist asking.

"I have a hunch I'll need a miracle," Andy said grimly. "That's off the record, though."

A junior member assigned to a losing case. Yes, that would save face for the established members of his outfit. Then why didn't he settle with WALCO, for heaven's sake?

"We'll go to the paper later," Andy said. "Let's go somewhere for that coffee, and we can kick the case around. Sure wish you were on my team, full time. I have an idea we could—"

"The newspaper first," Kim reminded him.

"Waste of time. I've already gone through everything in the morgue with a fine-tooth comb. Didn't learn much. Tell you about that, too, but let's get out of here, or your boss may come out of the house, change his mind, and spirit you back to the city."

He turned the ignition key, stepped on the starter, cocked his head, and listened to the engine. It coughed twice, then purred, and he grinned at Kim in delight.

"Hey, want to drive?" he asked. "Believe me, I don't let just anybody drive Victoria, but you know how to handle a clutch, with your little TR-four, so I'll trust you."

"Oh, I'd love to," she answered, eyes sparkling.

Andy got out and walked around to the passenger's side. Kim moved behind the wheel and gave a preliminary check: rearview mirror, side mirror, speedometer, gas and oil gauges.

"This is terrific." She grinned. "You sit way up high, almost like being in a little plane. Okay, boss, where do we go?"

"Just drive her around the back roads for a while and get the feel," he suggested. "The back country over the line in Connecticut would be good. Pretty scenery, too. Then maybe we can make it dinner instead of just coffee."

Well, why not? This wasn't like going off with one of those strangers Dan Aldrich worried about. Andy Hill was a reputable lawyer. An intriguing, attractive, complicated, and somewhat controversial attorney. Okay, call it a bona fide adventure without any risk.

They headed northeast to Greenwich, then northwest into the rolling hills and farmland, along narrow winding roads. They admired the autumn foliage and compared notes on their personal backgrounds.

Andy was an orphaned only child, but his father had been a lawyer. Her father was a lawyer. A common bond.

She had lived, briefly, in Puerto Rico, when her father was based there after joining the FBI. She'd like to go back. Hawaii would be fun, if her dad could ever be transferred there, and if WALCO would put her in the Honolulu branch office.

Andy had been born and reared in Hawaii, in Oahu. He had gone to the University of Hawaii, then come stateside to law school. Yes, he sailed and surfed. Loved the water. Thought he'd try snow skiing.

He sat halfway facing Kim, talking a mile a minute, asking questions about her life. Talking, she suddenly decided, to divert her attention from the fact that he kept glancing out the back window. She checked the rearview mirror.

Was that dark sedan following them? It was hard to tell. The road was narrow, and the driver might merely be trailing her because passing would be difficult. She slanted a quick glance at Andy, made up her mind suddenly, and swung off into a dirt road leading to a farmhouse. The sedan went on and vanished around a turn.

"Was that my imagination?" she demanded, breaking to a bone-jarring halt, then reversing and heading back to civilization. It was creepy, all of a sudden, to be way off here with an unknown man—a man who had persuaded her to leave the beaten path.

"Just some innocent man on his way home from work," Andy said casually.

Maybe. Maybe not. Kim was taking no chances; she was heading back to where there were people, as fast as she could. If she could. But she wasn't going to make an idiot of herself and let on that she'd had a bad moment or two, either.

She turned into the Boston Post Road and listened with half an ear while Andy gave her a running commentary. In pre-Revolutionary days, he mused, there were horse-drawn stages along this route. They left New York three times a week and took six days to make the trip, a grueling ordeal for the passengers. They stopped, en route, at wayside inns, had a light supper, and stumbled off to bed. Men and women, often strangers to each other, frequently had to share rooms. They were on their way again by 3:00 A.M. and traveled until 10:00 P.M.

"Um," said Kim, one eye cocked on the rearview mirror. Her pulse leaped.

There was a dark sedan behind them.

Take it easy, she told herself. *There are plenty of dark sedans in the world.* She gunned the ark she was driving. The sedan picked up speed.

5
post road
inn

"One of the Post Road inns, restored and in business, is just ahead to your right." Andy's voice slashed through Kim's preoccupation. "I'll watch for oncoming traffic. When I say turn, do it. Go right in between those sections of high privet hedge. Okay—now!"

They were going too fast. Victoria, top-heavy, careened wildly across the road on two wheels, then miraculously settled down on all four. They shot across a parking lot and came to rest in front of a long, sprawling log building not visible from the Post Road.

Kim's instinct was to leap out and run inside, but she had to see what happened to that dark sedan. Heart hammering, she watched the rearview mirror.

A dark sedan flashed past without slowing down. It disappeared from sight.

The girl's tight control snapped. "Now you can just kindly tell me what that was all about," she exploded. "Imagination, my foot! Just some innocent man on his way home! Pooh!"

"You're right; an explanation is in order,"

Andy agreed. "Come on inside. I'll buy you something cold and wet and tell you all about it."

It had better be good, Kim thought grimly. *Very* good indeed, or she'd find some other way to get to the train and home. Adventures were all well and good, but Kim wanted to know what was going on before she got any more deeply involved.

"I'm not playing in this ball game unless I know the score, friend," she announced as they went into the inn.

The interior was dimly lighted. The dining room, its tables set with snowy white linen and candles, was to the right. The bar, with heavy, hand hewn beams and dark paneling, was to the left. Andy chose the bar and opted for the last booth, where their backs were to the wall.

No one could walk casually past them, Kim noted, unless it happened to be a waiter en route to the kitchen. No one could listen to their conversation if they kept their voices low, except, again, a discreet waiter—or someone with a listening device.

Kim almost laughed at the way her imagination had taken off at a gallop. Andy, however, was not remotely amused. He looked furious.

"At least no one followed us into the parking lot," Kim said gratefully.

"Doesn't mean a thing," Andy answered. "Easiest thing in the world to go past, turn around, and walk in as casually as you please. We didn't get a close look at the driver—only the car."

"Then the car was following us!"

"I don't doubt it," Andy admitted. "I've had a tail a good share of the time ever since I went on this case. I figured it was just nuisance value, designed to throw a young, inexperienced lawyer off-balance. Matter of fact, I thought it was funny. After all, if I cared, I could quit driving around in Victoria and making myself conspicuous."

He lapsed into silence as the waiter approached to take their order. When they were served and the waiter was out of earshot, Kim asked why Andy had decided it was no longer funny.

"Because I don't want my girl involved in any sort of harassment, for one thing."

Kim's eyebrows shot up.

"I withdraw the statement," Andy said with a lopsided grin. "Counsel should refrain from making statements without first laying the proper groundwork." He leaned toward her, his eyes now serious. "Call that a bit of wishful thinking, Kim, but something I mean. I get this feeling that time is running out—on a lot of things."

The trial date had been set, he told her. It was only two weeks away, an amazing fact since the court calendar was so jammed that many cases were held up for months, even years. Normally, one would expect the plaintiff to be the one who wanted to hurry. The defendant, understandably, would like to postpone trial, hoping the plaintiff would be fully recovered, given sufficient time.

"Somebody got our case shoved up on the calendar," Andy said, "and it wasn't our side. What they're doing, whoever 'they' are, is rushing me, forcing me to go to trial without time to prepare."

"You've had a couple of months, haven't you?" Kim asked.

"No, that's the point." Andy said he had been on the case a scant two weeks. Another attorney had been retained by the Madden family, a man who had been a city judge. It was he, Judge Cranston, who had filed for the half million dollars, the exorbitant amount.

And then Judge Cranston had withdrawn and turned the case over to Andy's firm. "He said it was because he had a bad heart," Andy said, "Maybe somebody bought him."

"How? Why?"

Andy lowered his voice even more and glanced toward the door. "I don't want to wind up with a libel suit against me. I have no proof, just suspicions. A whole bunch of suspicions about all sorts of angles with this case."

Suppose, he suggested, that the former judge was, in truth, being paid to throw the case, much like a ballplayer bribed to throw a game. He sets up a losing case, enough money to prejudice the jury, and then drops the case. Perhaps the payoff is in money, perhaps in political patronage. Or perhaps he really is a sick man, who reached for a huge court settlement and huge fee, knowing it might be his last case, and then had a genuine coronary, too soon to try to collect. In any event, the case then went to Andy's firm.

"Who suggested your firm?" Kim asked.

"That's one of the peculiarities. Judge Cranston suggested it."

"And then your boss threw this losing setup to you, a relatively inexperienced trial lawyer?" Kim was shocked. "Does that mean collusion between the former judge and your boss? Is the whole world in on this deal? And why? Why?"

"I wouldn't like to think my boss was in on a setup," Andy reflected. "I don't really think so. I think he's honest, or I wouldn't be working for him. I think it's more likely that he figures a sort of trial by fire will make a man—a lawyer —of me. He's a tough old bird, Kim. Says he learned a lot from the cases he lost."

"Then, for heaven's sake, why don't you go along with Mr. Rydell and the out-of-court settlement?"

It really wasn't that simple, Andy explained. If the town of Neadham, the WALCO client, vetoed a settlement, it would be awkward for WALCO to go over the client's head—unless the company planned to drop the town as a client and lose a tremendous account.

"But Mr. Rydell said—"

"It's pretty involved, Kim. The suit is against the town of Neadham, not against WALCO. Granted, if the town loses, WALCO will have to pay, perhaps up to the amount of the total coverage. But no matter how hard Mr. Rydell tries to make my clients drop the suit, they're simply not going to do it. It's a matter of principle; they feel the town is at fault and they want to hit back."

"*Is* the town at fault?"

"I think so, or I wouldn't be handling the case. I'm sticking with the Maddens because *somebody* has to be on their side, on the side of justice."

Andy went on to tell her that the rock area had been open to the public during the past summer. Two of the lifeguards had told him so and had agreed to testify. The signs and ropes had been put up after Pete Madden's accident.

Furthermore, the rocks were supposed to be sprayed three times a week to prevent algae formation, to keep them from being slippery. The lifeguard said the money was supposed to come from admission charges collected at the turnstiles at the beach entrance. No spraying had been done all last summer.

"Can you prove that?" Kim asked.

"Only by the sworn testimony of the two lifeguards," Andy said. "And here's another peculiarity: The head lifeguard kept a daily log. Supposedly he wrote in, three times a week, that the spraying had not been done and that he had regularly requested it."

"Well, okay; subpoena the lifeguard and the log," Kim told him. "And, incidentally, where did the money go—the money from the turnstiles?"

"Don't I wish I knew. And don't I wish I had the time and a way to find out!"

There were plenty of other loose ends, he added. Why, for instance, had he been denied access to the town sheds in order to examine the spraying equipment and determine how recently it had been used? A laboratory analysis of spray nozzles might prove his point—if he had access.

And there was the case of the missing pictures. The two lifeguards said they had turned over pictures to Judge Cranston, pictures they themselves had taken of children playing on the rocks. No signs, no ropes. Cranston was ostensibly in an out-of-town hospital; his secretary maintained that there were no pictures.

"Oh, come on," protested Kim. "This is just too much—too blatant. The lifeguards will testify for you and—"

"Ah, but will they help? Oh, they'll try; they're willing to go out on a limb for justice. But— but all sorts of things are missing from the lifeguard station. Blankets, oxygen. Suppose someone is setting those kids up to be discredited as witnesses. Getting ready to accuse them, if only by innuendo, of thievery, so the jury will—"

"Then you just have to find the chief lifeguard and the log, for written proof."

"How? He seems to have vanished. Maybe he stole the stuff, for all I know, and skipped town. I doubt it, though. The other guards say the chief is an artist, that he's just gone wandering off somewhere to paint. They say they think he had received some sort of grant to study somewhere. They don't know where."

It was a big country. A big world. Plenty of places for a young man to study, if he had a grant. "What foundation gave him the grant?" Kim asked.

No one seemed to know, Andy admitted. The grant was only rumor, anyway.

"Well, we have to find out, one way or another," Kim said decisively. "Come on. You can have dinner at our place. If my dad's home, maybe he'll have some ideas of where we can start looking for information about grants for missing lifeguards. He can't do anything officially, unless there's reason to call in the FBI, but he might give us some ideas." *If he's home. The big "if."*

Andy agreed. They slipped from their booth and headed out the door. It was dark outside —not too dark, though, to notice a familiar-looking sedan parked near Victoria.

But it was dark enough that when the inn door opened again, a man was framed in the light showing from inside.

6
playing
"if"

"What are we going to do?" whispered Kim.

"Good question," mused Andy. He started to open the car door and help her in, then thought better of it.

Suddenly he snapped his fingers and doubled over with silent laughter. "Got it! Oh, good gosh, I'm going to fix a mix. Come on, girl, let's go back inside and. . . ." He leaned close and whispered in her ear.

Kim burst out laughing, too. Hand in hand, they raced back to the inn, unfortunately not in time to get a look at the man who had been watching them. He had faded away, so they still had no way of identifying him. Well, he was about to get his comeuppance. This was fun, turning the tables on him.

"Okay, Duchess, you're on stage," Andy murmured, summoning the maître d' with a peremptory forefinger.

Assuming her haughtiest air, Kim followed the man, flicking cold eyes over the few early diners, mentally filing their faces for possible future reference.

There were two couples seated together, hardly worth noticing because "their" man had been alone. Two middle-aged men, probably business associates, occupied a corner table. Only one man seemed to be alone. Mousy, nondescript, he had wispy, colorless hair, parted just above one ear and combed over the top of his head in a vain attempt to disguise baldness. Three garden-club-type women. Nothing promising.

Ah, well, Mr. No-face was going to get his lumps. Kim graciously permitted the maître d' to seat her where she could watch the lobby. Andy chose to sit beside her, rather than opposite, a normal idea for a couple tête-à-tête.

They studied the menu at length, as if they had all the time in the world. Let Mr. No-face fidget; served him right, wherever he was hiding —in the bar or in the walls. They gave their order at long last: lobster tails and tossed salad.

As the waiter retreated, Andy glanced at his watch and said casually, "If you will excuse me, I must make a phone call."

Kim nodded. She watched him go to the lobby and enter the last booth in a row of three, the booth against a partition. The other two booths were empty.

Now wait, someone was coming out of the bar, zeroing in on the phones. He was listing a bit, as if he'd drunk too much. Without seeming to sprint, Kim hurried to the middle booth and took possession, lest he try to listen in on Andy.

He's the one, she exulted. Tallish, thin, dark-haired, dark-skinned. Dark eyes, high-bridged nose. Pushing fifty years of age.

The culprit? No, drat! Merely bombed and trying to put change into a cigarette machine.

Kim called home, told Gerta she wouldn't be there for dinner, and found that her father was still away. She walked back to the table with Andy, knowing from the pressure of his fingers on her elbow that his mission had been successful.

"Might as well enjoy the meal," Andy said, seating her. "It'll take a little time to set things up."

Kim enjoyed it to the hilt. They left in precisely forty-five minutes, taking their time so Mr. No-face could follow. They climbed into the elderly car and drove off sedately. A pair of headlights trailed them at a discreet distance.

Then it happened. A long row of cars, parked beside the road, came to life. Headlights went on, motors coughed, then hummed. Thirty or so Model A Fords pulled out from the curb, surrounded Victoria, and swept her along in their line. Horns beeped in salute.

Kim collapsed with laughter. It was such a beautiful ploy, so absolutely marvelous and original. She could imagine the frustration of the person who thought following a classic Ford would be a lead-pipe cinch—until an entire Model A club arrived on the scene.

Andy's gang entered into the spirit of the lark with a vengeance. One car would pull off into a side street and go tooling away, then another. Who could tell if one special car remained in line? As a matter of fact, Andy himself cut out of line, went around a block, and passed the cavalcade going in the opposite direction. He finally headed for New York.

It was the sort of lark to delight the soul of Kim Aldrich, and then, abruptly, it wasn't really so funny after all. No one was following them now, true, but there were questions to be asked —and answered, this time, instead of being adroitly sidestepped or ignored.

"Okay, now what's this all about? Nuisance value, harassment, you said. Sure, but there must be more to it than that. Tell me," she demanded.

"I honestly thought they were just heckling —whoever 'they' are. Now I have to admit—"

"Admit what?"

"I have no facts, only suspicions. Nothing that would stand up in a court of law."

"Oh, come on, Counselor," Kim said impatiently.

"Look, suppose they're sticking to me like glue, trying to get something on me."

"I'm not sure I read you."

"Well, look, suppose they got to Cranston, one way or another. Money perhaps, political patronage possibly. Or a threat, some danger he wants, above everything, to avoid. He plays ball, sets up a losing case. Enter Andrew Hill.

"Sounds safe for their side. But safe isn't positive. They—whoever they are—can't afford the smallest loophole. This guy Hill might pull a miracle out of the hat, somehow turn the tide. They keep quiet during the trial, as long as Hill is acting like a loser.

"But comes that miracle, just possibly. Then, outside the courtroom, someone approaches Hill, puts the squeeze on him, tightens the thumbscrew. Result: Hill throws the case. Easy enough to do, because the cards are already stacked against him."

"What could they get on you?" Kim asked. "You haven't accepted a bribe. You haven't done anything wrong, anything that might result in your being disbarred, have you?"

"There are other levers that can be used against people." Andy banged the steering wheel with his fist. "Blast!" he exploded. "I'm a fool, Kim, an absolute *fool*. No, I haven't done anything wrong except to forget to use my head, except to drag you into danger."

"Me?" Kim had cast her lot with Andy. She felt wonderfully safe with him.

"Be serious," Andy ordered. "A threat to my family would bring me into line, make me obey orders. I have no family, no wife. But how about if they find I'm in love? Well, then, a threat to my girl, and presto!"

Lovely, oh, lovely to have him admit, even if obliquely, that he loved her! But too soon to admit that she, too, was on the brink of falling in love, too soon because the relationship was too young and delicate for declarations.

"A threat to you," Andy groaned. "How could I let you, or any other girl, wind up in danger? I mean, how could I live with myself if I subjected even a total stranger. . . ."

Kim was catapulted from Cloud Nine. She picked up the pieces and said, "That's silly. You're a lawyer. They must know the first thing you'd do is go straight to the police."

"That, my dear child, is a beautiful theory," Andy scoffed. "In real life, in the cold, cruel world, people are far more likely to do exactly as they're told, avoid the police like the plague to protect someone else. Oh, sure, I'd make like a hero and report a threat to myself, but to jeopardize someone else's life—well, now, that's a different kettle of fish."

"You wouldn't throw a case, no matter what!"

"How do I know what I'd do if it came to the clutch?" he growled. "It would be one devil of a decision to make, that much I do know."

"You're playing 'If,' " Kim said. "Okay, I can play 'If,' too. If you can win your case, you go ahead and win it. If I'm in danger, I can take care of myself. But if you could just find that chief lifeguard— Listen, Andy, you said yourself that time is running out. Well, then, why don't you hire a private detective to track down that missing chief?"

"That runs into dough. I don't have that kind of drawing account. It'd probably have to come out of my own pocket," Andy mused. "I thought I had months to work up my case, but we're down to days. Days!"

"I could . . . help," Kim offered. "I mean, I— well, I have a little money and—well, darn it all, right is right, and I *want* to help."

It was a mistake. Her timing was wrong. She should have been more subtle. Now she'd gone and offended his male pride. Oh, stupid, stupid! But she did want to help!

"No!" Andy exploded. Then in a quiet voice he added, "I have a feeling that it wouldn't be quite ethical, since you're an employee of the insurance company involved."

"Right is right," she repeated stubbornly.

They were driving along Shore Road, past Travers Island, summer headquarters of the New York Athletic Club. The lagoon, opening off the Sound, stretched from the Athletic Club to City Island Causeway and was marked in lanes, with ropes and lemons, for the use of college racing crews and Olympic tryouts. Kim had been here often, watching the sleek, beautiful racing shells.

Long Island Sound to port, a winding, quiet road ahead, a golf course and riding academy to starboard. And a parking lot to the left, just beyond the Athletic Club. Andy swung off here, braked—and took Kim in his arms.

She could hear his heart pound, or was it hers? Only one thing was wrong: He let her go as suddenly as he had kissed her, and she had to fight the urge to cling.

"What was that for?" she whispered. *Oh, say it; say it was because I'm really your girl!*

"That was for thanks," he said roughly. "Thanks, but no, thanks, Kim. I mean that."

He backed around, headed back to Shore Road, crossed the drawbridge. On to the Cross Bronx Expressway, to the Triboro Bridge, to the FDR Drive, to the Ninetieth Street exit. South on Park Avenue to the East Seventies. All the way, Andy was sitting right there beside Kim, but he had gone away, and she couldn't find him and was desolate.

It was a silent stranger who parked the venerable Victoria on the treelined street and got out to help his passenger to alight. A doorman beat him to it, assisted Kim, and then withdrew discreetly.

"Will you come up for a nightcap?" Her vocal cords were tight with strain, and she had to force the words out. What had happened to the easy repartee, the shared laughter that needed no explanation?

"No," Andy said coldly. "You'll be perfectly safe as long as your place has a doorman. Please excuse me if it seems rude to leave you in the lobby, but—"

"Will I see you soon?" she asked painfully, in a low voice.

Astonishingly, insultingly, his voice was loud enough to be heard for half a block. "No, I hardly think we have any reason to meet again, Miss Aldrich. You mean well, but you have no right to meddle in a case that doesn't concern you. I suggest that in the future you stick to your typing and filing and—"

Intolerable! Unbelievable! Tears welling in her eyes, Kim spun around and rushed inside her building.

She didn't see the dark sedan parked a few cars down the street. She didn't see Victoria pull out from the curb, followed by a dark shadow.

7
meet
mr. no-face

He doesn't have to be in love with me, but he doesn't have to be so brutal, either, Kim raged inwardly as she rode up in the elevator. *Who does he think he is?*

More important, who do I think he is? An attractive, weather-beaten-looking man. Likes the things I like—sports, adventure. Wild sense of fun.

Lawyer. Honest. She was sure of that, even if she was furious at him. Dedicated to justice.

Rude. Yes, but rudeness was out of character. All right, then, why rude? Worried, that's why. Worried about Kim Aldrich for some vague reason, right or wrong. Or stubborn enough to prefer to handle problems alone, smart enough to know how to chase a girl right out of his life.

But suppose the girl was every bit as stubborn. Suppose she refused to be dismissed and insisted on helping. Then she stood a good chance of being humiliated again. Unpleasant prospect.

Right is right, however. Kim knew she was

not going to bow out and leave Andy to the wolves.

Her mind was made up by the time she put her key in the lock of the Aldrich apartment; she was going to help Andy if she possibly could, whether he liked it or not. How? That remained to be seen.

Tom's flight bag was on the floor, just inside the door.

"Anybody home?" she called. Foolish question. Someone was *always* home to greet Kim, a fact that sometimes rankled because it meant she was still the baby of the family. Tonight she was glad of the company.

"In the kitchen, mini sister," Tom answered.

An amazing sight met her eyes when she went to join him. Newspapers were spread on Gerta's spotless floor. Gerta and Tom were on their hands and knees, trying to coax a little ball of fluff, a reddish little pup, to drink from a saucer of milk.

Kim got down on the floor, too, her heart melting. The pup, tail wagging, came over and, with brown eyes, begged her to love him. His new slave picked him up, cuddled him and crooned over him. He licked her right ear enthusiastically.

"Oh, Tom, where did you get him?" she asked.

"It's not a him, it's a her." Tom grinned.

"Found the poor little thing just wandering around in the parking lot out at the airport, poking around, trying to find something to eat. Or, rather, she found me. She fell in step and trotted along beside my left foot. I tried and tried to shoo her off, but back she came, wagging her tail. Figured at first that she had tumbled out of a car when someone got out to go meet a plane.

"Now I think someone deliberately dumped her off, hoping that somebody would come along and adopt her," he added.

"That's a horrible thing to do to a defenseless animal." Kim bristled. Even if a family couldn't afford to feed a pup, they could always leave it at an animal shelter.

"Yes. Well, I took her back inside and put a call on the public address, notified the police, even called the radio stations. The consensus is that she was abandoned. She has no collar for one thing, and the way she sneaks food, but won't eat if anyone's watching her," Tom explained.

He should have turned her in at one of the shelters himself, he went on, but hadn't because he felt responsible. Instead, he had taken her to a veterinarian, ordered rabies and distemper and liver shots, and brought her along home.

"She tried to sit on my lap all the way," he

said. "Poor little thing. I'll find one of the guys at the field who'll be willing to adopt her, someone with a house and kids."

"Couldn't we—" Kim began, her heart in her eyes.

"Darn, I knew I never should have brought her," Tom muttered. He went over and tousled his sister's hair affectionately. "You look about twelve years old, mini sister. Like the kid who pleads, 'He followed me home. Can I keep him?' This is an Irish terrier, Sis, according to the vet. Terriers have to dig. This little spook needs a yard to play in."

Bloomp went Kim's heart. They had talked this over many times, she, her brother, her father, and her sister. No dogs, they had agreed, not as long as they lived in an apartment. It wouldn't be fair to a dog.

But they had been talking about a theoretical dog, not this adorable and adoring moppet.

Pete! Pete Madden, she thought suddenly. Inspiration. Pete was cooped up, trapped, lonely. He *needed* a puppy. Yes, that's *exactly* what he needed.

If only Mrs. Madden would agree. The house had a yard. Pete might be persuaded (persuaded!) to sit outdoors on sunny days and watch the puppy play. Surely his mother would agree if she really cared about the boy.

Tom agreed it would be worth a try. She'd

have to go to the Maddens' alone on Saturday,
though; he'd be off on another flight.

"I don't mind going alone." Kim's answer
was a masterpiece of understatement. Mind?
She honestly wanted to do something to help
Pete. And, she admitted, she wanted a reason
to keep in close contact with the principals of
the Neadham case. Mostly, though, she really
wanted to see Pete's eyes light up, see his
thoughts turn outward.

If she'd been thinking clearly, she would have
gone out and bought a puppy for Pete anyway.

"She can sleep in my room," Kim announced.

Gerta produced a cardboard carton for a
bed. They lined it with soft towels. "We need,
now, an alarm clock to wrap and tuck in with
the puppy," Gerta said. "The clock ticks, just
like the mama dog's heart, so puppy is not
afraid."

Tom and Kim looked at each other and
laughed. "Progress," Tom remarked. "There isn't
a single, old-fashioned, windup clock in this
entire place. Every one runs by electricity. No
tick."

Gerta, however, produced one from her room,
a clock she had brought from her homeland and
considered far more dependable than anything
new. "This was the only one that worked in the
blackout, that time when there was no electric
power in the city."

The pup slept beside Kim's bed. Little orphan, still without a name, so Pete could have the privilege of chosing one. Little No-name.

Mr. No-face.

Kim shivered in the darkness. When someone followed someone else, there was usually a lot more to it than mere harassment. Someone was playing for keeps.

Kim was up at the crack of dawn to put the collar that Tom had bought on little No-name and take her for a walk. Then she changed her clothes and went to work early, hoping she'd have a chance to discuss the Neadham case with Mr. Rydell.

An odd thing happened soon after she arrived at the office. A special delivery letter came for her. It was an offer of employment, a glamour job as secretary to the manager of a resort hotel in Puerto Rico. Her passage would be paid; the salary was nearly double what she earned at WALCO; she would have full use of hotel facilities; etcetera, etcetera, etcetera. Kim had never heard of the outfit.

Why in the world would they want me, of all the secretaries in the world? How would they even know my name? Well, she'd look them up when she had time, just for fun. Probably someone who had known her father in Puerto Rico.

She dropped the letter into her purse and

forgot about it, because Mr. Rydell arrived. If she got to him before the day's business took his attention, she might be able to discuss the Neadham case. She was in luck; her boss was willing to listen.

She told him about Andy's suspicions, about the man following him, about her own questions.

"Wouldn't it be possible for WALCO to put an investigator on it, have someone find that missing chief lifeguard?" she asked at the end of her dissertation. "Doesn't it seem warranted, when this seems to be a case with—with criminal connotations?"

Mr. Rydell studied his fingertips for a long time, then studied his secretary. "Facts, Miss Aldrich," he said gently. "You have no facts at all to support a theory of crime behind the scenes."

"But—but—" she sputtered.

"No facts; only hearsay. You *heard* Mr. Hill's tale of intrigue and crime, a story he could have built out of whole cloth, for all you or I know. If he had proof of any crime, it would be his duty to report it to the proper authorities."

"But don't you see that it's all wound up in the case he's working on?" she pleaded. "It's *part* of his case. And—and anyway, that car following us wasn't hearsay. I saw it with my own eyes."

"Did you get the license number? Make? Model number? Year? Description of the driver?"

Kim colored. "No." No to all those questions.

"Well, then." Mr. Rydell spread his hands, palms up. "There's really nothing we can do, Miss Aldrich, except to continue to support our client, the town of Neadham."

"But the money from the turnstiles—where did it go? And how about the beach, the rocks that should have been sprayed but weren't, and the ropes and signs put up after the accident—"

"Hearsay, Miss Aldrich, still only hearsay. But questions like that can be brought out in the trial. If Mr. Hill has proof, he can accuse. I should imagine the town has adequate proof of innocence, however. My advice to Mr. Hill is to avoid a libel suit by not accusing unless he has absolute, airtight proof.

"And as for you, Miss Aldrich, I must also caution you. Don't repeat any of these suspicions, or you might be involved in a libel suit yourself. Now then, I think it's commendable that you're so interested, and I have no objection if you do some amateur investigating on your own time, but—"

He didn't believe her suspicions were well grounded. He never had, and there was no way to make him believe. He had encouraged her to do some sleuthing to make her feel a part of the company, important, less apt to change to another job! Hah! He was on the side of the client all the way. Closed mind.

"It's a fine thing to be young and all fired up with enthusiasm for a cause," Mr. Rydell went on. "In this instance, I'll be glad to listen to any more theories and, naturally, any facts you might turn up. I shall, however, prick holes in your ideas if I can, because that will help you sift fact from fancy. I don't mean to be unkind, but merely helpful, because one day you may settle on a career as an investigator for WALCO."

She wasn't going to open her mouth again, she vowed, until she had facts or an airtight theory. So far, she had to admit to herself, she was talking in circles, trying to clarify vague fears and suspicions. And she'd also keep the puppy and the proposed visit to the Maddens to herself, rather than risk ridicule or, even worse, a direct order to drop the plan.

She went to Neadham the next morning, the puppy in a box on the right-hand bucket seat of her TR. A case of dog food and some puppy biscuits were stored in the trunk.

She made the mistake of going by way of Shore Road, past the place where Andy had stopped to kiss her. It made her feel desolate—and nervous enough to keep looking in the rear-view mirror all the rest of the way.

It was weird the way every car that came up behind her seemed to be a dark sedan. Kim really couldn't tell one conventional car from another. Her interest lay in sports cars, and she recognized practically every one on the road, but even if last night's shadow car pulled right up beside her, she knew she'd never be sure it was the one.

It was a relief to reach the Madden house at last, even though she was uncertain about the kind of a reception she'd receive. She had considered phoning ahead and asking permission to come but decided against it. Once confronted with the fact of the woolly little dog, Mrs. Madden wouldn't have the heart to say no —Kim hoped.

"Come on, doglet," she crooned, scooping her little charge up in her arms. "And if they don't want you, I'll just keep you myself. Maybe I'll persuade Dad to buy a house in the suburbs and call it the Dog House. Or maybe I'll just have to take that job in Puerto Rico, live in a guest cottage, and give you a yard to play in."

She rang the doorbell, sure that she heard sounds of scurrying inside. No one answered. She rang again and waited. And waited. Probably while Mrs. Madden put Pete in bed, if he had been up in the wheelchair.

Eventually, the door opened. "Yes?" said a tallish, thin man. "What do you want?"

Kim stared, tongue-tied. She knew him—at least she had seen him before. Dark eyes, high-bridged nose, perhaps in his late forties. The man in the Post Road Inn, the one who had headed toward the phone booth and, instead, had put some coins in the cigarette machine. He gave no sign of recognizing her.

"I—my name's Aldrich, Kim Aldrich," she stammered. "I was here on Thursday. I—"

"You from town? Did Commissioner Saunders send you? Why?" he demanded.

"Oh, no, no," Kim said. "I'm a secretary at WALCO, the insurance company. I—well, I just wanted to see Pete. I promised I'd keep tabs on him."

"Well, I don't know," the man said doubtfully. "I'm his father, see? Our lawyer said not to let anyone in unless he's here, too."

The puppy solved the problem. She squirmed in Kim's arms and gave a small yip.

"Dad," yelled Pete. "Daddy, who's there? Is it a puppy? Is it for me? Can I see it now, please, *please*—"

So. This was Mr. Madden. He shrugged and motioned for her to follow him to the back bedroom. Mrs. Madden was there, looking as harried as before, as she tried to keep Pete from struggling to an upright position in his bed.

"Miss Aldrich, oh, Miss Aldrich!" the boy

squealed, holding out his hands. "Is he mine?
Can I keep him? Can I, *please*?"

"Mind your manners," Mrs. Madden said.

"Is it all right?" Kim begged, looking from
one adult to the other. She wished she hadn't
sprung the surprise, because if they said no it
would tear Pete's heart out.

Who could resist such an adorable, cuddly
ball of fluff? Not the Maddens, thank goodness.
They melted as Kim put the puppy carefully on
the bed.

"What's his name?" whispered Pete, practically holding his breath in delight as the dog
worked its way up to his shoulder, then licked
his ear.

"It's a little girl dog," Kim explained. "She
doesn't have a name yet. She's an orphan."

There was a sudden feeling of tension in the
room, something almost tangible enough to
touch. Kim caught a glance exchanged by Mr.
and Mrs. Madden. Pete missed it completely.
The puppy was now in his arms, and a look of
pure bliss spread over his face.

What in the world? Why should the parents
freeze up in— In what? Fear? Because it was a
female puppy? Ridiculous; a female pup was a
better pet for a family, especially for an injured
child. More affectionate, more home loving.

Orphan! Yes, that's what had done it, Kim
thought.

Mrs. Madden: tall, thin, dark-haired, dark-eyed. Mr. Madden: tall, thin, dark-eyed. Pete Madden: stocky build, freckles, red hair. Well, it was possible. No, it wasn't. Hadn't Kim learned in biology that blue-eyed children do not result from the union of two dark-eyed parents?

No, no, no; that was backwards. Two blue-eyed parents could have only blue-eyed children. Was that it? What *was* it she had read about dominant or recessive genes? Well, anyway, Kim was positive the boy was adopted. The question was, Did Andy Hill know? Did *Pete* know?

How awful, how perfectly awful, if the adoptive parents made the mistake of keeping the information from the boy. How traumatic if he found it out suddenly, without warning.

Suppose Duncan MacKenzie, attorney at law, discovered this. Might he not use it to convince a jury that the parents were opportunists? Wouldn't the jury, at least some of the jurors, believe that adoptive parents were more apt to "use" the child than natural parents?

Andy Hill ought to know, for the protection of his clients—even if she had to swallow her pride and phone him, and even if he laughed in her face and assured her he had seen a copy of Pete's birth certificate and that he wasn't adopted at all. He *was* adopted. Kim knew it in her bones.

"I'm going to name her Sparky," Pete said, interrupting Kim's train of thought, "because she has such sparkly-brown button eyes. I'm going to write to Bill and tell him all about Sparky."

"That's nice," Kim murmured.

"Bill's my friend," Pete announced importantly. "He came to help me when I got hurt at the beach. He was the chief lifeguard."

Dear Lord in heaven, Kim prayed wildly, wondering if she could believe her ears.

"I'm going to be a lifeguard when I grow up. Like Bill and Don and Ricky and—" Pete's voice broke, and he buried his face in the puppy's soft coat. "Only I can't; I can't ever—"

"Pete," Kim pleaded in a high, unnatural tone, "honey, please. Do you know his address?"

Tell me, Pete. Hurry. So I can tell Andy, and we can get a statement and win your case, and —and you'll be able to afford the best doctors in the whole world.

"Whose address?" mumbled Pete.

8
missing
witness

"This Bill, the chief lifeguard. Do you know where he lives?" Kim pleaded, frantic now.

Five wasted minutes might be too long. Andy might go away for the weekend in just that time. The lifeguard might move again, disappear all over again. By the time they could trace him, the trial might be all over.

"Of course I know where he lives," Pete said. "How else could I write to him?"

But you're only seven years old, Kim thought. *Are you just making all this up, pretending to be grown up enough to write letters? Oh, I couldn't bear that.*

She turned to the boy's parents, beseeching. "Do you have the lifeguard's name and address, Mr. Madden, Mrs. Madden? Oh, please. That lifeguard is the most important witness for your trial. *Your* witness, don't you see?"

How could they see, when she kept babbling like this? Kim took a deep breath and began again. "Your lawyer, Mr. Hill, says that the chief lifeguard is the one person who can prove —*prove*—that the rock area was never sprayed, that people were *not* told to keep off. That lifeguard is the miracle Mr. Hill has been praying for."

"How come you're so anxious to help?" Mr. Madden asked. "You work for the insurance company. You wouldn't want to see us collect for the kid's injury. What's your angle?"

"Oh, for heaven's sake!" Kim said impatiently. "My company—I— We are interested in justice. If your child was the innocent victim of negligence on the part of town officials or, worse, of criminal action—" That was a mistake. Never, never accuse without proof. Too late to take the words back, though.

"I want to help, can't you see?" She was begging now.

"I'll get the letters," Mrs. Madden said. "The lifeguard has written several to Pete, and I helped Pete write back."

She went out of the room. She was gone forever, it seemed, and Kim had a nightmarish feeling that the letters were missing. Maybe, somehow, this evidence had also been destroyed.

"Here," Mrs. Madden said, coming back and handing Kim several letters held together with a rubber band. "The address is on the outside of the envelopes."

And the name, too, Kim saw. W.J. Jones, c/o General Delivery, Santa Elena, California.

All right, she said to herself, *so it isn't the*

*perfect clue or the absolute answer, but it's a
start.* They'd find him, and, of course, they'd
contact him. In time for the trial, too. They'd
get him here—and the logbook, too, because he
had to have that log—even if she had to pay his
plane fare herself.

"You can read the letters if you want," Mrs.
Madden said diffidently.

Kim snatched the earliest one from its envelope, along with a color snapshot of a red-haired
young man with a wide grin.

"That's Bill," said Pete.

> "Dear Pete," Kim read.
> "Sorry I couldn't get in to see you while you
> were in the hospital. Just wanted to let you
> know I tried and that I'm thinking of you and
> hoping you'll soon be up and around and good
> as new.
> "A crazy thing happened to me. I was given
> a fellowship to work on my painting. It works
> like this: A big outfit gives money to people—
> art students, writers, and like that—so they
> can study and learn without having to worry
> about money for a year or so. Get it? Like last
> summer, I worked at the beach so I could eat
> and have a roof over my head, but the job
> didn't leave me much time for painting. Didn't
> know how I'd manage after the beach closed
> and the job ended.
> "Then this Dier Foundation—"

Kim gasped. This was the real miracle, the
name of the foundation! The foundation people would be able to contact Bill pronto.

"Then this Dier Foundation sent me a letter and offered me a cabin in the mountains in California for a year and enough money for food. Can you imagine that? Right out of the blue, they offered this, and I hadn't even applied for help. Don't even know how they heard of me. Maybe somebody at the beach saw me painting on my day off or something.

"Anyway, Pete, I had to grab the chance before they changed their minds. That's why I didn't have time to see you.

"Keep your chin up. Write and tell me how you're making out. Best of luck. Your friend, Bill."

Bill sounded nice—exuberant about his own good fortune, naturally, but concerned about a small boy who had been injured, concerned not only about his physical welfare, but about making sure the boy knew his friends cared about him, concerned enough to help, Kim was sure.

"Could I take this letter, just borrow it to show to Mr. Hill?" she asked the room in general.

"No," Mr. Madden said suddenly, snatching the packet. "No, if this is important, it stays here."

"You're right," Kim said, startled. "Yes, you're right. Don't give them to anyone at all, anyone except Mr. Hill. Put them away somewhere safe. Don't tell anyone—except Mr. Hill—a word about them."

She didn't want them with her because—

well, of course it was ridiculous, but Andy *had* said she might be in danger. She wouldn't even write down the name and address or the name of the foundation. She'd remember them and tell Andy.

"Could I use your phone? I want to call Mr. Hill," she said.

"I already did," Mrs. Madden said. "Tried to get him when I went to the other room to get the letters. He's not home. I—almost didn't let you see the letters," she said apologetically. "I wanted to ask him if I should. Then I had to decide, and I decided to trust you. I mean, you brought the puppy and all—"

Thank goodness, Kim thought. Thank Tom for the puppy, who was now sleeping, cuddled up against Pete. Thank heaven for Mrs. Madden's decision.

She was frantic to leave, to find Andy. But how? He could be anywhere at all; it would be like looking for a needle in a haystack. But she had to start somewhere. She could go to his home perhaps and find out if he had a landlord or a neighbor who might know where to locate him. She could unearth one of his classic-car-club buddies—something, anything.

She did know Andy Hill's address and his telephone number. She had looked them up while she sat by the phone at home, hoping he'd call. Several times she had started to dial, wanting to hear his voice and recapture the magic, but she had fought the impulse. She was not, repeat *not*, going to chase him.

This was different. Now it was vital to his case that she talk to him. She'd go to his house and wait until he came back, if necessary— even if it took until Monday.

"Bill's going to win the money for us," Pete said suddenly. "He'll come and help us, and we'll be rich."

Oh, dear. Kim's heart sank. "Try not to think about it," she advised lamely. "Mr. Hill and I will work on finding your pal Bill. We'll all do our best."

"Bill will come," Pete said flatly.

Kim could have kicked herself for talking in front of the child, for raising his hopes. She knew better than that, too, but she'd been completely carried away with excitement. That was no excuse, though.

"I'd better be on my way," she said, leaning over and rumpling Pete's hair affectionately. "I'll see you soon."

The boy pulled the puppy close, hid it with his arms. "You're not going to take Sparky, are you?"

"No, honey; Sparky's your dog." Someday, though, she was going to live in a house with a yard and have a dog. Amazing how it hurt to part with the pup. "I brought some food for

Sparky," she said. "It's out in the car. I'll go get it."

"I'll go with you and carry it in," Mr. Madden offered. Apparently he, too, had decided to accept her.

Ah, yes, but Kim had certain reservations about him. She couldn't think of a single reason why Mr. Madden would have been following Andy, perhaps working for the enemy, but he *had* been at the Post Inn. And he hadn't let on that they had met practically face-to-face. Coincidence? Her father had taught her to be suspicious of apparent coincidence; it usually was planned.

On the way out to the car she fumbled for a reasonably diplomatic way to question Mr. Madden, then gave up and bluntly asked, "Didn't I see you at the Post Road Inn the other night? Thursday."

"Now I get it," answered Madden. "Thought I'd seen you somewhere but couldn't place you. You were the girl with Mr. Hill. Right? Well, I was on my way home, saw his car pull into the parking lot. Thought I'd stop in, buy him a drink, and see if he was making any progress on the case. Saw he was with a dame—excuse me, girl—so I went into the bar alone. Had one too many, too."

"You didn't happen to see anyone following Mr. Hill, did you?"

No. Kim knew it even before he said so. That would have been too much luck for one day. No point in crying about it. She had other things to do, starting with finding Andy Hill.

She took the dog food from the trunk and handed it over. "Maybe you'd better take the box from the front seat, too," she suggested. "The puppy slept in it for a couple of nights." Not that Sparky would sleep in any box if Pete had his way; the pup would be in his bed. "There's a sock with a knot in the toe. The puppy likes to throw it around and pounce on it ferociously."

Cutting short Mr. Madden's thanks, Kim slid behind the wheel of the TR and started on her mission. She already had a fair idea of how to reach the peninsula extending out into Long Island Sound, where Andy lived. She had already studied a road map and marked the spot.

Getting there was confusing because there were few through streets. Via a series of turns, two stops to consult her map, and a bit of luck, she eventually drove between two stone gateposts bearing the legend, ORION POINT.

"Whew!" Kim whistled. This was a genuine estate area, private. A narrow road led toward the end of the point, past enormous homes, each with a gate at the entrance of its private drive. *Whew and double whew! It must cost a fortune to live here,* she mused. Had Andy Hill inherited a fortune, or what?

The road was ending, leading into the last estate. For a minute she thought she must have made a mistake and come to the wrong place entirely, but she drove up to the last pair of stone gateposts. The name, THE PRIORY, was chiseled into the top of one.

Baffled, she braked the TR, got out, and pushed some vines from two rural-delivery-type mailboxes. PRYOR proclaimed one, in black printing. HILL announced the other.

Kim had only two alternatives; either turn around and go back, or drive between the forbidding gateposts. She chose to go in, trying to stifle a queasy feeling. Anyone—she or Andy—who was followed here would be boxed in; there was no alternate route out, except by boat or a cold swim.

At her left were several acres of dense growth, a natural woods. Ahead and slightly to her right, past a lawn and shrubs, was a huge, dark-stained house with leaded windows. It was situated on a bluff, high above the Sound. The view would be spectacular at any time, but what a wild, remote place it would be during a storm!

It was a millionaire's house—or had been at one time—the sort of place a wealthy family used only in summer. In winter they'd go to their Caribbean or Mediterranean home.

Kim stopped the car and sat there with the

motor idling, trying to figure out the enigma of
Andy Hill and this imposing place. Then her
face cleared and she laughed. She had been so
overwhelmed that it had simply not registered
when she saw a carriage house just inside the
gates, to the right—a converted carriage house
with a brass knocker and the name "Hill."

Now it all made sense. Andy rented these
digs. Actually, it was exactly the sort of spot a
man who drove an unconventional car would
choose. It was also the kind of place that appealed enormously to one Kim Aldrich—or
would, under normal circumstances. The ab-
normality of the circumstances was thrust upon
her by the sound of a car approaching. The hair
stood up on the back of her neck.

Kim put her car in neutral, killed the engine,
and rolled silently down a small grade. The little
TR4 slid neatly between two stands of dense
spruce. Heart pounding, she waited.

She had seen no sign of people in the big
house on the bluff, no life in the houses along
the road before the gates. If she shouted, would
anyone hear her—anyone except the driver of
the car coming toward the Priory?

9
information,
please

Victoria lumbered through the gate and came to rest in front of the carriage house. Kim, weak-kneed with relief, tried to catch her breath and figure how in the world she could come out with some semblance of dignity.

Andy Hill climbed out of his vintage vehicle, stared at the ground for an instant, looked her way, then dashed into the trees. He grabbed the girl and spun her around.

Kim knew an instant of blind panic. Who was the enemy? Was it Andy himself? If so, and there wasn't another person for miles around—

"What in blazes are you doing here?" he shouted, shaking her like a rag doll when she tried to break loose and run.

"I—I—came to—to find—to tell—" she gasped.

"To find me? To tell me something?" he roared, giving another shake for good measure. "And hide in the bushes just to make sure you — You crazy little fool! Don't you know I might have brought out a gun and shot into those trees? I have a permit to carry a weapon, in case you're wondering if I mean it."

"How did you know I was there?"

"Tire tracks."

"You're hurting my arm," she said plaintively.

"Sorry." The pressure eased, but he didn't let go. "Guess I'm a little jumpy these days."

"Then why in heaven's name do you drive around in a car that can be so easily followed?" she demanded. "Why live way out here at the end of nowhere, with no escape route? Seems pretty stupid to me."

"Seems even more stupid to let someone force me to change my way of life," he snapped. "At first it was sort of funny, and I thumbed my nose, in effect, by driving Victoria. Now maybe it's not so funny, but I don't intend to be— People can follow me on public streets, but this is private property. I can have trespassers arrested."

His grip tightened on her arm. "And speaking of trespassers, you still haven't told me what you're doing here, why you were hiding. Tell me. And it had better be good or I *will* have you arrested."

Kim was shocked. "You don't think I'm—that I'm—" She couldn't even say it.

"Playing on the other team? The thought crossed my mind," he said dryly. "I trusted you, told you entirely too much. It was a mistake.

Yes, I was concerned for your safety and sorry I had brought you into the picture. But you could have been a plant. As Mr. Rydell said you would, you did pick my brains."

"Oh, but—oh, *no*," she wailed, horrified. It was okay if she suspected him; call it caution. Then why was it so outrageous when he suspected her? Because—because it just was, that's why.

There was no time for any childish defense. She hadn't come here to win a popularity contest; she had come to pass along some vital information.

So get on with it. "I can prove I'm on your side if you'll just listen. You have to listen, Andy. It's important, no matter what you think of me."

He allowed her to go inside his domain. The enormous living room had dark wood walls— the originals used in the carriage house—and a heating system that was obviously an afterthought, tacked on when the owners decided to rent the place for year-round use. The ducts were suspended from the ceiling, so low that a man of Andy's height had to duck his head when he crossed under them.

"Sit there," said the host, pointing to a leather bucket chair. He stood in front of her, looking down, reserving judgment.

Kim bounced back up onto her feet, too excited to stay put. Once started, the words tumbled out: disjointed fragments of the puppy episode, the reason for her trip to Needham— and the clincher, the discovery of the name and address of the chief lifeguard and the name of the foundation that had given him the grant.

As the explanation babbled out, the Lord High Executioner changed back into Andy Hill, friend. "Out of the mouths of babes," he said in wonder. "Kim, you're a genius. Kim Aldrich, Girl Detective."

"Shucks, it was nothing," she said airily. Grinning ruefully, she added, "This particular Girl Detective has an unfortunate tendency to scare herself witless. But, come on; let's *do* something to get started finding that Bill Jones."

"Yeah, give me that name again, the town, and the name of the foundation." He rummaged in a pocket, pulled out a beat-up envelope and made notations. Then he loped the length of the room, where bookshelves covered the entire wall.

"Atlas first," he mumbled, extracting a volume and opening to California. "Santa Elena, hm. Population five hundred. Okay, now hand me that phone book so we can compare the map inside the cover with this one and find the area code. Okay, seven-one-four, right?"

He reached for the phone on the desk and dialed "directory assistance" for that area.

"What city please?" said a cheerful-sounding voice. "Santa Elena? What name, please?" The cheerful tone became one of regret. "I'm very sorry, sir, there is no listing for William Jones in Santa Elena. Is there some other name for the listing?"

"Uh, no. No, wait. Could you give me the number of the post office, the postmaster?" Andy covered the phone with his hand, winked at Kim, and murmured, "Best detectives in the world, these telephone company gals."

Kim was practically dancing up and down in her impatience. She tried to listen in. It was quite natural for Andy to put an arm around her shoulders and draw her head close to his.

The number was produced.

It was not a postmaster who answered the call, but a postmistress, a by-the-book postmistress. She was very sorry but she couldn't give out any information. Even if she knew where Mr. Jones was living, even if she personally knew of a neighbor with a phone, it would be impossible for her to divulge. . . .

It was useless; she wouldn't budge.

"Now what?" asked Kim, still in the circle of Andy's arm.

"One stab at finding the foundation. Just pray it's in New York, because we can't call 'information' in every city in the country—or in the world," he answered, dialing.

Another cheerful-sounding voice became a voice of regret. There was no listing in Manhattan for the Dier Foundation.

And even if there were, Kim pointed out, this was Saturday, and the foundation offices would be closed. Oh, what frustration! They were stymied, at least until Monday, and probably even then.

"Let's go to the public library and see if they have any information," Andy said.

"Phone; it's quicker," Kim urged.

Negative, negative. The librarian could find no reference to a Dier Foundation. Oh, yes, yes, indeed; they had many volumes listing various foundations, other volumes dealing with grants available for artists, writers, musicians. Oh, yes, indeed. But no information about a Dier Foundation.

"Try the *Daily News* Information Service," Kim said on sudden inspiration. "They know everything about everything." She had phoned there often enough to know the number by heart.

The *Daily News* Information Service was closed on Saturdays—and Sundays—and holidays.

"Telegram? Can we send a wire?" Kim asked.

"To General Delivery?" Andy asked. "Search me, but it's worth a try. They'd have to put it with Jones's mail, I suppose. Wouldn't get to

him any sooner than an airmail letter, because
he won't be able to pick up his mail until Monday, anyway."

"Maybe he only comes into town once a
week, maybe once a month, for his mail," wailed
Kim. "Oh, I can't stand this. I just cannot bear
it."

"Seems like a letter is our only hope," Andy
said dejectedly. "Okay, then, the sooner we get
it written and mailed, the sooner he *might* get
it."

He produced a portable typewriter, rolled in
paper and began to write, hunt and peck. Kim
pushed him aside.

"I'm a secretary, remember?" she said. "You
dictate; I'll type. I can take it down directly on
the machine, if you don't go too fast."

"Good girl; and, as long as you're an expert,
make me a carbon copy for my office files."

Andy dictated efficiently, organizing his
thoughts quickly, talking at an even pace, giving a concise picture of the Madden case as it
stood on the eve of trial. He explained that he
wanted Bill Jones to come East to testify as to
whether or not the rocks had been sprayed during the summer and whether or not the rock
area had been posted as off limits.

"If you have any information as to how the
funds from the turnstiles were used, this also
would be most helpful to us," he went on. "If

the logbook is in your possession, please bring it. If not, can you tell us where to locate it? I assure you, that log is vital to our case.

"The boy's injuries are certainly real, and he is, in my estimation, entitled to redress. As things appear to date, he may lose his case. This would be a gross miscarriage of justice, in my opinion."

Andy closed with an urgent appeal to the chief lifeguard to phone collect to Andy's office. They could then arrange the details of Bill Jones's trip East. Andy would pay for the flight.

Andy signed the letter in a bold scrawl, folded it, and inserted it in the envelope Kim addressed. He sealed it, affixed stamps, and, with a red marking pen, labeled it "Air Mail" front and back. "That about does it," he said, "except for posting it."

"Then let's get on with it," Kim urged. "Let's take it right to the post office— No, wait. Why don't I take it to New York and drop it at the main post office on my way home? It might save a whole day." She held out her hand.

Andy tapped the letter against the edge of the desk, studying her thoughtfully. He did not relinquish the letter.

"You still don't trust me." Kim was stung.

"Let's say I've been struck by a somewhat delayed attack of caution, or perhaps a recurrence of a previous attack."

"Then you take it," she flared. "Only just don't stand there wasting time."

He relented and handed over the letter. She was almost too furious to take it—almost.

"Simmer down, Kim," he advised. "People who are angry often fail to think clearly. Now get going. I'll follow you until you get on the Thruway to be sure nobody's tailing you."

"Now who's not thinking?" she challenged. "You're the one with the car nobody can miss, the one who's being followed. You'd only call attention to me. And, as long as we're on the subject, suppose you tell me, once and for all, *why* you're being followed. You never did really explain."

He assumed, he told her, that the opposition —the "they" in the case—wanted to keep a close eye on him to find out exactly what information he was digging up, whom he was interviewing, and so on. For all he knew, he might be getting close to something vitally important, perhaps related to his case, perhaps much bigger than his case.

"Like what?"

"Money, perhaps. Crime. Corruption. Who knows? The question still remains about what happened to the money from the turnstiles. That must be a fat sum. And there might be other fat sums from other parts of town—the swimming pools, for instance."

"Why don't you just go to the police?" Kim asked. The minute the words were out, she knew they were foolish.

"Evidence," Andy said. "We have suspicions but no E-V-I-D-E-N-C-E. If I had proof of a crime, I would report it. Anyway, my immediate concern is the Madden suit. If, in preparing my case, I unearth evidence of crime, I'll go right to the district attorney. Meanwhile—"

"Hey," interrupted Kim, "I almost forgot. I think Pete Madden is adopted. I'm sure of it."

Andy snapped his fingers. "I should have thought of that myself. Nobody mentioned it to me, though. They didn't tell you? You just guessed? Well, it does bear looking into. I'll ask them, point-blank."

Now maybe he'd trust her. She had come up with something he'd missed, something he considered important.

"I'll drop in on them and check it out after I see you on your way," Andy said. "Let's go, but you be careful, hear? If 'they' begin to suspect you're a very nosy little girl who might stumble on something, 'they' might find some way to remove you from the action."

That was silly, Kim tried to tell herself, but if enough money was involved, if a big enough crime operation was hidden in the background, she might indeed be removed. By the offer of a job in Puerto Rico? Or—

She shivered. Things "happened," strange "accidents" that the FBI sometimes proved were staged. Oh, yes, this could be a very real thing, not a figment of imagination or a television thriller. There had been several such "accidents" right here in Westchester County.

She could take it from there and build a real horror sequence. Someone follows her from here, Andy's home, to the post office. Someone watches her put a letter into the slot, the *airmail* slot.

It wouldn't be hard to guess whom the letter was going to—especially if Bill Jones had been removed from the scene by the mysteriously opportune study grant that took him to California.

And then, with Bill Jones again constituting a threat, he would be removed permanently. Well, wouldn't he—if he held the key to something enormously important?

And if Kim Aldrich didn't stop following this line of reasoning, she'd scare herself to death.

"What's the matter?" Andy cut into her train of thought. "You look as if you'd seen a ghost."

He wasn't too far wrong, but there was no point in admitting it, or he'd push her out of the action, somehow, for her own protection. She shook her head. "I'm okay; just impatient to get the show on the road. I'll even agree to let you baby-sit me to the New England Thruway, only let's go, let's go." *Before I lose my nerve again*, she added to herself.

She drove her little red TR through Neadham, followed by Victoria, beeped her horn in farewell, and drove up the ramp to the New York artery of the Thruway. And now she was on her own. She had asked for it.

Even the sky seemed suddenly ominous. A dark cloud bank moved in and obscured the sun. Kim glanced in the rearview mirror, half expecting to see a dark sedan right behind her.

"You can stop that right now," she said aloud. "You make a heck of a rotten detective, that's for sure. Even if someone had the magic powers to read your mind and know where you were going, how would you be able to spot your tail in this stream of city-bound traffic? What do you expect to see, a car with a big sign saying, 'Following Kim Aldrich'? So stop being so stupid, and keep your mind on your driving."

She turned on the radio for company and caught a weather report. A storm was moving in, she learned, but it was not expected to hit the area full force for several hours. Meanwhile, flights out of Newark, LaGuardia, and Kennedy Airports were leaving on schedule, but passengers planning on late departures were advised to check with their airlines before leaving home.

Airports! Of course! And if she hadn't been so busy scaring herself witless, she'd have thought of that before. It was silly to take such an important letter into Manhattan, where it would have to be sorted from among millions of other letters, then taken to Kennedy Airport, and *then* put aboard a plane.

The logical thing to do was take it to Kennedy herself, Kim decided, and mail it there. It would save hours, perhaps a full day. She'd switch over to the Hutchinson River Parkway, take the Whitestone Bridge across the East River to the Whitestone Expressway, then the Van Wyck Expressway, and be at Kennedy in a half hour—exactly as anyone pursuing her would expect, she thought uneasily.

10
calculated
risk

Kim killed Sunday. She talked Gerta into going to a movie at Radio City Music Hall and having dinner out.

There wasn't one blasted thing she could do about the Neadham case until Monday, and she knew she'd only get another spell of the jitters if she hung around the apartment. Granted, nothing had happened when she mailed the letter out at Kennedy, but it spooked her to think how easily someone could have followed her. Maybe someone *had,* and she just hadn't been alert enough to—

That kind of thinking could lead to a blown mind, she scolded herself, hustling Gerta out the door, down in the elevator, and into a cab.

She didn't remember a thing about the movie or the stage show after they left the Music Hall. They took another cab to La Cave Henri IV, a wonderful little cellar restaurant in the East Fifties. It was one of her favorite spots, with its informal Parisian atmosphere. Tonight it depressed her. Something about the candle-light reminded her sharply of Andy and started

her worrying about him all over again. Hah! As
if she had ever stopped.

She practically rushed poor Gerta through
her meal, into yet another cab, and home. She
had a horrible feeling she shouldn't have gone
out at all. Suppose Andy had tried to phone
her with some important news—or just to
talk.

There, I knew it, she thought in dismay as
they left the elevator and she fumbled for her
key. The phone was ringing inside. *I knew it, I
knew it. Oh, drat this stupid key.*

It didn't have to be Andy, of course, but it
could be an important call, nonetheless. It
might be her father, Tom, or Cindy. Or Andy.

She flung the door open, hurtled through, and
dove for the phone. The line was dead. Someone
had just hung up, just this second. And now
the dial tone mocked her.

"Whoever it was, he will call back," Gerta
said comfortably.

Yes, yes, of course. Well, it couldn't hurt to
hurry him a bit, Kim decided, ringing Andy's
number. There was no answer.

She tried to read, tried to watch TV, then
gave up. She took a shower and went to bed.
Surprisingly, she slept like a log and woke up
Monday morning raring to go. This time, she
told herself as she rode downtown in the subway, she had a few things to tell Mr. Rydell,

and this time he was going to listen—*and* do something about it. He wouldn't brush off her information about the chief lifeguard and about the possibility of Pete Madden's being an adopted child. He'd *do* something.

He actually did do something. Mr. Rydell took notes, said he'd pass them along to the investigator, and encouraged her to take time to contact the *News* Information Service and try to locate the name and address of the Dier Foundation.

On impulse, she showed him the letter offering her the job in Puerto Rico.

"You're not thinking of leaving us, are you, Miss Aldrich?" he said, raising an eyebrow. "We'd hate to lose you. I have a feeling that you might have the makings of an investigator yourself, given time.

"Of course, I wouldn't want to deny you a real opportunity," he continued. "However, I do urge you to look into this proposition carefully before you make any decision. Any change of jobs entails a certain amount of risk, but make sure you calculate the risk."

Mr. Insurance himself was speaking, Kim thought impatiently. The field of insurance was, of course, based on the calculated risk. A company could afford to insure a home against fire damage, for example, because not every home was going to have a fire. For every claim paid, there would be thousands of insured homeowners who would never have occasion to submit claims. Thus, some of the money paid in for insurance was, after operating expenses, profit.

Kim's father would have expressed his doubts differently. "Look before you leap," Dan Aldrich often told her.

"That's the point, Mr. Rydell," Kim said. "I don't know a thing about this hotel. I never even heard of it before, and I wouldn't know how to look into it. Not that I want to leave WALCO. I don't; but I *am* curious. Andy—Mr. Hill—thinks maybe someone just wants me away from the Neadham thing."

"Hmm. Well, then, give it to me, and I'll have Chris Townsend look into it."

That suited her fine. She scooted back to her desk to call the *News* Information Service.

Negative. The researchers found no record of the Dier Foundation. She called Chris and enlisted his aid. An hour later he phoned back.

"Nothing, Kim," he reported. "I came up with a Greer Foundation, but nothing even close to Dier. Tried transposing and looking for *D-e-i-r*. No soap. Sorry, but thanks for tipping me off. It may stack up to something in the overall case. Incidentally, I'm checking out the Puerto Rican thing."

"Dier," Kim mumbled. "Spelled like 'die.'" She shuddered. *And you, my girl, should take that*

*vivid imagination of yours and turn it in on a
new model,* she told herself. *Find one that
doesn't keep you ready to jump right out of
your skin. Or leave the insurance field completely. Go back to college and major in botany.
Spend your life learning to grow beautiful flowers and perform grafts—* Graft!

Even flowers would be unsafe for a person
with her leanings, she thought, grinning. Wasn't
it Cornell University that had an entire demon-
stration garden devoted to the growing of poi-
sonous plants? As a botanist, she would in-
evitably wind up specializing in just those plants
—and being called in on murder cases.

At least the Neadham thing wasn't a murder
case. Not yet, anyway. At that, they wouldn't
really know for sure until they found Bill
Jones.

She phoned Andy's office to tell him the news
about the Dier Foundation. He wasn't there. His
secretary said Mr. Hill was in court.

She hadn't stopped to realize that the Nead-
ham-Madden case wasn't the only thing Andy
might be working on. And, she reminded herself
sternly, it wasn't the only one she was supposed
to be working on, either. Unless she wanted to
be a *former* secretary, she had to get busy and
type up a few jillion forms and letters and reports.

Andy returned her call in the late afternoon.

He received the information on Dier glumly. "And they pushed the Madden case up again," he said in a flat tone. "We go to trial on Thursday. *This* Thursday."

Kim gasped. "How can that be possible?"

"It can. It is."

"Then ask for a postponement."

"What do you think I've been trying to do all day over at court?" he snapped. "Sorry; I didn't mean to snarl at you, but it's just—just—"

"Frustrating," Kim put in. "Frightening. Yes, I know. You haven't heard from Bill Jones?"

"Too soon for that."

Or too late, Kim thought, wondering how she could endure the agony of suspense—with time passing inexorably—wondering if they would hear from Bill Jones in time. Wondering if he would come in time. Wondering *if, if, if.*

She endured the rest of Monday, all of Tuesday, and all of Wednesday for just one reason: She had no alternative. If kicking and screaming and banging her head on the wall would have helped establish contact with Bill Jones, she would gladly have kicked, screamed, and banged.

The jury was selected on Thursday. Mr. Rydell went to White Plains, the county seat, to observe the selections in the State Supreme Court building. He did not take his secretary along, so Kim had to endure Thursday, too.

As an act of defiance, she sent a telegram to William J. Jones, c/o General Delivery, Santa Elena, California. It didn't ease her tension. It produced no results.

It was evening before she heard anything. Andy called her at home. He was anything but elated at the selection of jurors.

"We have two men who may be on our side," he reported. "Madame Foreman—well, she's anybody's guess. She may be sympathetic, but, again, she may have suffered an injury, received no recompense, and become bitter. Or she may be smug and righteous because she didn't bring suit; therefore nobody else can be justified in bringing suit. Or maybe her suit was defeated and she's going to get revenge."

"But, if you can count on a possible two, even one to vote for Pete—"

"This is not a criminal suit, Kim; it's a civil suit. A unanimous decision is not required in a civil action. Two votes wouldn't be enough. We need a minimum of four, and that wouldn't win—merely hang the jury. It takes a three-quarters vote to win."

The picture was blacker than Kim had realized. "No word from California?"

"No," he answered bleakly. "Tomorrow we make our opening statements, and we'll have to start taking testimony. I feel as if I'm going to the guillotine."

She tried valiantly to provide moral support. "You're articulate, Andy, and you believe in your case. My boss says there's a rule of thumb that jurors and judges are automatically sympathetic to an injured child, that an award is almost always made in favor of a child."

"Not if the deck is stacked against the child," he said bitterly.

"Did anything else happen?"

"Yes. I used up all my challenges, but somehow, call it a freak stroke of luck or fate or something, *somehow* it turned out that every last one of the jurors is a homeowner."

"What's that got to do with it?" Kim asked.

"Maybe nothing, but the Maddens rent. Homeowners consider renters as transients, sort of second-class citizens who bear none of the burdens of taxation and so have no real rights," Andy answered.

"That isn't right. Sure, I know the landlord pays the taxes, but the renters really pay them, because they come out of the rent money. Rents are high in high-tax areas. Just ask my father. Our rent—"

"True, technically, but try to get any homeowner to believe that," he scoffed. "No, sir, they feel they're carrying the renters. And now a renter, a transient, someone who contributes nothing—in the estimation of the owners—comes along and sues for an enormous sum, takes the money, and goes back under a rock or something."

"It's really that bad?" she asked.

"Psychologically it could be. Listen; try to persuade Mr. Rydell to take you along to court tomorrow. I'd like your opinion of the jurors. Sometimes a woman's intuition— Well, anyway, see if you can swing it. Then watch the jurors' faces during the opening statements, during testimony. I know it's clutching at straws, but—"

Kim promised to do her best to be there.

"Try to get some sleep," she suggested gently. "Things will look brighter in the morning."

"Platitudes! As for sleep, what's that?" He sounded exhausted. "Oh, by the way, you were right; Pete is an adopted child. He doesn't know. They feel they have a legitimate reason for not telling him."

"Does anyone else know, except us?"

"Not that I know of. The Maddens have lived here only a year, and the boy was adopted in infancy." Then, saying that he had to get back to work on his opening statement, Andy rang off.

Kim lay awake for hours that night, her mind running in circles. Why, she wondered, if there was corruption in the town government, did they want to risk going to trial and possibly being exposed?

Well, first of all, the town did not want to pay out one cent. An out-of-court settlement might have been made in an amount covered by insurance. Yes, but word would get around, and other suits might result. Then the insurance rates might go up.

Not good enough. Okay, then carry it one step further. An increase in insurance rates might well be reflected in a tax increase. Then what? *Then* the residents would rise up in wrath and vote in a new administration. Yes, that could be it! Once out of office "they" would lose not only prestige and salaries and expense accounts but also their access to graft and to funds that could be embezzled.

That seemed logical to Kim. It could be reason enough to take the calculated risk of going to trial. Not a blind risk, but one in which every possible loophole had been plugged.

And they must be pretty sure of themselves— might even have an ace up their sleeves. What ace? Only time would tell, but Kim was sure of one thing: She simply must be in court tomorrow. She must find some way, short of quitting her job, to persuade Mr. Rydell to take her.

She dreaded asking him in the morning. To her amazement, Mr. Rydell fully approved of her interest.

"I'll just take a quick glance at the mail," he said, "and then we'd better leave. We'll go in my car. Chris Townsend will join us down at the parking lot in—" he glanced at his watch— "in fifteen minutes. Court convenes at ten o'clock."

That hurdle surmounted, Kim arranged for another secretary to take her place, took a few minutes to brief her replacement, and was ready and waiting when Mr. Rydell came out of his private office. He carried a slim attaché case containing the WALCO file on the accident case.

They traveled via the Major Deegan Expressway to the county seat. Luck was with them; they found space in the Main-Martine Avenue four-tiered parking area a block from the courthouse.

The Supreme Court building was imposing, with broad steps that seemed to Kim to rise practically forever. Kim was further impressed as they entered a vast marble rotunda.

The elevators were to their left. They rode up, then walked along a corridor to a door marked V and called, in legal parlance, "Part Five." This was where the case of Madden vs. the Town of Neadham would be heard.

The spectators' section was filled, except for the front benches. Kim sat in the front row at the right of the aisle. Mr. Rydell and Chris would join her here after they conferred briefly with Duncan MacKenzie, attorney for the defense.

Kim glanced around briefly, taking in the high bench with the flag at one side. The witness stand was directly at the right of the bench, the jury box still farther to the right, against the wall. A long table in front of the left section of the spectators' area was reserved for Andy Hill. Counsel for the defense was already at his table, in front of Kim.

The Maddens, white-faced and drawn, entered and sat at the left of the aisle. Andy Hill pushed Pete in, in his wheelchair, and settled him out of traffic. Andy's eyes lighted when they met Kim's. Pete looked too terrified to recognize her.

The poor baby, she thought. *Look,* she wanted to say, you're *not on trial; it's Neadham that's on trial.*

The jurors filed in. The uniformed guard closed the doors and took up his position before them. The bailiff went to the front of the room.

"Hear ye, hear ye, hear ye," he intoned. "State of New York Supreme Court, Part Five, now in session, Judge John Casey presiding. All rise."

As everyone stood up, a portly man in a black robe entered, took his place, and banged his gavel. The trial had begun.

Andy Hill's opening statement was a straightforward account of the facts of the accident. He said he would prove the cause: negligence on the part of the town of Neadham in failing to make the rock area safe through the use of anti-algae spray. An area, he said flatly, open to the public until after the accident.

It was a good speech, ending with an eloquent plea for justice for a small boy who had been needlessly crippled. Kim was proud of Andy; his sincerity shone in his eyes.

Then Duncan MacKenzie delivered his statement. He was a big man with wide shoulders and an air of total confidence. He was dynamic, brilliant, and cold as ice. He glittered.

He compelled the jury to listen as he painted a picture of an accident-prone child.

Kim's heart sank.

"I will show you, ladies and gentlemen of the jury, I will *prove* to you that this is not the first accident that Peter Madden has sustained."

All children have accidents, Kim thought in anguish. *They fracture arms when they fall out of trees or off bikes, they—*

"Now, what happens to cause a child to be accident-prone? We know, we can prove with psychological evidence beyond reproach, that one cause can be a home environment that is utterly disturbing to a child."

Counsel for the defense glanced significantly at the Maddens. They turned ashen.

"A child in such an environment becomes so insecure that he is too nervous to anticipate and avoid danger. Or, worse, he becomes so unhappy that he has a subconscious death wish."

Oh, monstrous, monstrous. Kim groaned inwardly.

"The child is an innocent victim. He is not to be blamed. I welcome this opportunity to bring things out in the open. You, ladies and gentlemen of the jury, are going to have the privilege of helping this child. It is not money that he needs. He needs professional help, and, by the time this trial is concluded, the proper authorities will be able to take steps."

He knows. Kim wept silently. *He knows about the adoption. He's going to use it ruthlessly.* He would twist everything and pull the world out from under Pete. *Diabolical!*

11
cat and
mouse

Kim was completely drained by the time court was recessed. Her ordeal was intensified by the way Duncan MacKenzie played a cat-and-mouse game around the adoption, never coming out and saying it, but alluding to a fact he would bring out in testimony.

The adoption was his ace up his sleeve, she was sure. He was going to use it when it would count most, at the end of the trial, in his summation. He would drop it—like a bomb.

She didn't even try to talk to Andy after the session. White-faced and grim, he left with his clients, and there was no point in trying to catch up. She had nothing to offer in the way of encouragement.

What could she report about the jurors' reactions? Only that there were two young, athletic-looking men who seemed sympathetic to Pete when Andy described his injuries. And that the entire jury had been hypnotized by the brilliance of Duncan MacKenzie's oratory!

She rode back to New York with Mr. Rydell and Chris, sitting huddled in a miserable heap

135

in the corner of the backseat. She listened in silent agony while her boss and the WALCO investigator recounted every insinuation, every dramatic gesture of the famous trial lawyer.

"And if it hadn't been for all the interruptions, he would have been even more impressive," Chris remarked.

Kim had been glad each time the bailiff had approached the bench, whispered to the judge, and given him a note or a verbal message. The judge had scribbled an answer on several occasions; twice he had called ten-minute recesses and left the courtroom. Each time it had seemed like a small reprieve, and Kim had prayed that Duncan MacKenzie would be thrown off stride and the spell he had cast upon the jury broken.

Now she had time to speculate on the reason for all those interruptions. It reminded her of something. If only she could collect her wits and dig it out of her memory.

When had she heard of—yes! Yes, it was her own father who had appeared before a judge who received a series of messages. It had soured Dan Aldrich enough to leave his law practice and go into the FBI.

Such messages, her father had said, are not proof of collusion, but they should alert everyone to the possibility. In her father's case, his opponent was sending offers of a bribe if the judge would swing the case in the opponent's favor. The judge could do so, if he were without conscience, by overruling objections, deliberately slanting his charge to the jury, and all but coming out and telling them how to vote.

Kim's spirits hit rock bottom. It was sickening to face the possibility that Judge Casey was capable of accepting a bribe.

"People will do anything for money," Commissioner Saunders had said. *And*, Kim thought grimly, *he should certainly know*.

"Everyone has his Achilles' heel," was the way Andy had expressed it when he had admitted that concern for her could be used as a club against him.

There seemed to be a giant conspiracy. Andy and his clients were being gobbled up ruthlessly in order to—to what? To cover something evil! They shouldn't be allowed to get away with it, Kim decided. Somebody had to do something!

Who?

"You, Kim Aldrich," she answered herself.

"I beg your pardon; did you say something?" Mr. Rydell asked.

"I—no," she said, covering herself with a fit of coughing.

Okay. What can you do? she challenged herself silently.

Go to California. Get the chief lifeguard. Bring him back to appear on Monday as a witness. That's what. It was such a simple, logical solution that she could have kicked herself for not thinking of it sooner. It wouldn't even cost her anything for her own ticket; her brother could get her a pass. The rest—Bill Jones's fare, a car rental, and whatever—could just come out of her bank account, money she'd saved since she'd been working and bonds her father had given her on birthdays.

Oh, no! A sudden thought brought her up short. The banks were already closed. Tomorrow was Saturday; they'd be closed all weekend. Monday would be too late. Monday, she would have to tell her boss, her family, everybody in the world of her plan in order to get time off from work. And they'd say no, individually and collectively.

That let Tom out, too, as far as asking him for a loan. She'd have to be devious, as it was, to get a pass without telling him her real reason for wanting it.

All right. Another obstacle has been placed in your way. Are you going to let that stop you, Kim Aldrich? Not on your life, she answered herself. *This is the credit card age. Remember?* With an airline pass and her credit card, she could go practically anywhere in the world.

It was Friday, and Tom was home. He could have had a date but, for once in this nightmare, luck was on Kim's side. And Tom was highly amused that his sister wanted to dash off to California for a weekend. Amused, but cautious enough to ask her why.

"Well, you know my roommate from school lives in Pasadena," she reminded him. "I just thought it would be sort of great to pop out and —" It was an evasion but not an outright lie—a necessary evasion, even if it did go against the grain.

Tom thought about it too long to suit his sister. "Well, okay, if you don't want to get me a pass, see if I care." She forced a grin to go with a bit of impudence. "Gerta wants to go visit her sister this weekend. I don't mind staying here alone. It was your idea, yours and Dad's and Cindy's, that I needed baby-sitting."

Tom laughed. "The whole idea of a trip to California sounds to me like a plot. A girl's backward approach to getting her own way and staying alone in the apartment. Right? Well, I'm going to call your bluff. You're *going* to California, even if I have to put you aboard the plane myself."

"That won't be necessary," she assured him, primly.

"No, it won't," he said agreeably, "because I'll check with the crew to make sure you've boarded the plane."

Kim decided not to push her luck and make an issue of her dislike of being forever taken care of. She'd better say no more, or he might get it into his head to phone her former roommate in California and check on her arrival. That would blow her plans sky high.

She was at Kennedy Airport at 10:00 A.M. on Saturday. Her flight was scheduled for a 10:30 takeoff, so she had time to arrange for the rental of a car in Los Angeles. She also picked up a California road map.

So far so good. As soon as she was inside the stretched-out DC 8, her carry-on bag stashed under her seat, she took the road map from her purse. She would figure the route to Santa Elena and not waste any time once she reached the West Coast.

Her seatmate settled down, fastened his safety belt, and leaned over to look at her map. It made her skin crawl to discover a stranger so interested in her destination. She folded the map and crammed it back into her purse, took out a paperback book, and pretended to read.

Now she was trapped for hours, perhaps sitting right beside someone whose job it was to follow her. It was too late to change to another flight, too late even to phone Andy or tell anyone at all where she was bound, because they were taxiing out to the runway. The jets screamed. The giant silver bird was airborne.

Now, for the first time, Kim had time to assess her situation. The more she considered it, the more she was faced with a bitter fact: This was no calculated risk she was taking; she was rushing off, heading into the unknown. She hadn't even taken the precaution of telling one living soul where she was going. She must have had rocks in her head.

Yet, what else could she have done? Someone had to do something to reach Bill Jones, and fate seemed to have appointed Kim Aldrich. Even so, she decided dismally, she had certainly embarked on her mission in a foolhardy manner.

She kept her face turned away from her seatmate and stared down at the retreating ground; then she heard someone talking. She recognized the voice. It was Andy Hill, asking the stranger beside her if he would mind changing places. Almost faint with relief, she turned to him.

His expression was so grim that she had a fleeting thought that Andy himself might be the one assigned to keeping tabs on her. Ridiculous, of course, but still—

"You crazy little fool!" he said when he was seated.

"How did you find me?" she asked.

"Easy. I phoned your home and talked to your brother. He even told me what flight you were on. I was lucky that there was still space, or I'd have had to bump someone or catch an earlier plane and meet you in L.A."

"You didn't tell my brother why—where—" No, of course he hadn't, or *she* would have been bumped.

"It would have taken too long to explain," Andy said. "By the time I could have told him what I thought you were doing, you'd have left." He was furious.

"I'm glad you're here," she said meekly. "I thought that man you just changed places with was following me."

"Maybe he was, for all you or I know," Andy said. "It wouldn't matter to him if he didn't sit beside you. In fact, it might throw you off your guard if he didn't. After all, you can't go very far away in the next five hours, unless you have a parachute hidden somewhere." His tone softened a little. "I should have made the decision myself to go to L.A. But it was a fool thing for you to tackle alone."

"I only wanted to help," she said in a small voice. "Don't be angry at me."

"As a matter of fact, you can make me madder—and, yes, I mean mad, insane with worry —than anyone I ever met in my entire life. I ought to turn you over my knee."

"Can't." She grinned. "There isn't room. But if you try, I'll—I'll fasten my safety belt."

"You, Kim Aldrich, are incorrigible," Andy said ruefully. "But not expendable. You remember that, you hear?"

"I didn't know you cared," she said flippantly, hoping he'd say more.

He did. He said he would tell her exactly what she meant to him, once they were free of the stress. First things first, meanwhile.

She could wait, now that he had given her an inkling, now that he held her hand firmly in his. She could forget the Neadham case for a few hours, too. She could pretend they were on a honeymoon, going all the way to Hawaii on this flight, so he could show her where he grew up, went to school, and went surfing. Then she could picture him as a little boy and feel that she really knew him.

It was a lovely dream while it lasted.

It came to an abrupt end when they landed and went to the rental counter to pick up the keys to the car Kim had reserved.

"Aldrich?" said the baffled girl behind the counter, shuffling through reservation orders. "There seems to be some mistake. We had a reservation in that name, but it was canceled."

"Canceled?" Kim was dumbfounded.

"I'm the guilty one," Andy said, stepping into the breach. "You see, my—my fiancée made the reservation, and I didn't want it to go on her credit card. I made a reservation in my own name."

The girl was glad to have that confusion cleared up. "Your name, sir?"

"You don't have it," he said with a disarming grin. "I always deal with the number-two rental outfit, the ones who try harder." He winked.

The girl smiled lingeringly at Andy and turned to another customer.

"Did you really cancel me out?" Kim asked as Andy led her away. "I had an idea you were every bit as surprised as I was. Do you honestly have another reservation?"

"No, yes, and no, in that order," Andy answered. "No, I did not cancel you out. Yes, I was surprised. No, I have no other reservation."

Kim stopped dead in her tracks. "Suppose you explain what this is all about. It seems to me that I've been in a state of complete confusion ever since—ever since I met you. I don't understand half of what's going on."

"That makes two of us. About all I know is that I smell a rat—a rat named Saunders. I don't even know exactly how he figures in all this mess, but I do know he's ready to commit perjury on the witness stand. And that I have to be able to call him on it."

"I still don't get this thing about the car," Kim persisted.

Andy took a guess. Suppose someone at the other end of the flight, the East Coast, decided not to follow Kim himself. Suppose a West Coast shadow was engaged.

How was the West Coast character supposed

to recognize Kim? Obviously by hearing her name. "Okay," Andy went on. "Now, our guy can't be in three places at once so he takes up a position in a central spot where he can watch. With a little luck, he can see one girl who seems to be having difficulties. She doesn't just pick up her keys and sign. The clerk searches, explains. Girl looks baffled. Girl fits description. Drift close, verify the name when she asks to have her reservation reinstated."

"How would they know which car rental I had dealt with?"

"No problem at all," Andy explained. "First, it's logical to assume you would rent a car, any car. Okay, they start with the so-called number-one outfit. They want to cancel out Kim Aldrich. Heck, they wouldn't even have to get a woman to call to cancel a woman's reservation. Kim could be either a girl's name or a man's name, for that matter. And how many car rental companies are there? Not many. Start at the beginning. Wrong one, no record of Aldrich reservation? 'Oops, sorry; my brother or father or sister must have made the reservation with XYZ Company.' 'That's perfectly all right, sir; thank you for calling.' Get it?"

"I get this," Kim said. "I get the fact that you think someone *is* following us—me. Meanwhile, here we are with no wheels and with time running out. What do we do now?"

They'd have to take their chances, Andy decided. Oh, they'd try to throw any pursuers off the track. Kim would go to one rental counter and ask about rates, just talk awhile. Andy, meanwhile, would go to another and rent a car. Then they'd drive around in L.A. for a bit, double back, and finally get on the San Bernardino Freeway. It wasn't the most brilliant scheme, he admitted, but it was the best he could dream up at the moment.

It wasted valuable time and made them both nervous, but Andy knew his way around Los Angeles. After a dizzying series of turns and circles, they entered the Freeway. Once there, they had no way to tell if they were being followed, with so many hundreds of cars.

Kim's eyes began to burn.

"Smog," explained Andy. "It's really a goofy system, everybody driving around in cars, no public transportation at all. No matter how New Yorkers may gripe about the subways and commuter trains, it's better than this. The only way people *can* get to work from the outlying areas out here is by car."

"Why don't they put in commuter trains?"

"The mighty oil companies say no. They are not about to lose such an enormous source of revenue. They swing a lot of weight politically. Result: John and Jane Doe and all the little Does have to breathe exhaust fumes—or move."

Now that she had had time to think, Kim was impressed by Andy's logic in explaining the cancellation of her car. She told him so and added that she was glad he was along, because she would have been a sitting duck all alone.

"Sometimes I scare myself." Andy grinned. "Sometimes I think I'd make a better criminal than a lawyer, because I can figure exactly what I'd do if I were on the other side."

Kim laughed. That didn't mean he was cut out to be a criminal, she assured him. It meant he could see into the criminal mind and be a better lawyer. Had he considered criminal law?

They were approaching their exit, ready to head toward the desert—ready to give up their feeble attempt at lighthearted banter. There was an arroyo to cross, and a narrow, twisting road to navigate.

A car roared up behind them, crowding, crowding. Andy fought the wheel, careening wildly. The door on his side popped open, and he was gone.

Kim had fastened her seat belt. Why hadn't Andy? she thought. Then, just before her head crashed against something and she blacked out, she recalled little Pete Madden's words: "I thought I was going to heaven."

12
scratch
one witness

Kim's head ached. It was splitting wide open, she was sure. Someone was pounding her head with a sledgehammer.

Off in the distance, a girl mumbled. Something about Andy. "It was you," mumbled the voice. "All the time it was you, Andy. You're the one, and you tried to kill me. Why, Andy? Don't you want to win your case? Or are you being paid off?" The voice became plaintive. "I thought you loved me, Andy. Why would you try to kill me? I was only trying to help." Then the voice rose shrilly. "I can't see! I'm blind!"

The voice was her own. Kim reached out in stark terror.

Strong arms held her. "Don't move," Andy said hoarsely. "Don't move because you might injure— Oh, Lord, why did I ever let you get mixed up in— Kim, Kim, darling, I didn't try to kill you. I love you."

Andy loved her. Then everything was all right. Kim opened her eyes and laughed hysterically. "Always remember to open your eyes if you want to be able to see," she said.

148

"Don't move," Andy begged. "I'll get a doctor, an ambulance, somehow. This is the time I'd give my right arm to have a phone in the car. Always thought anyone with a phone in the car was a show-off, but—"

"I'm all right," Kim murmured, her head on his shoulder. "Just let me stay here for a minute."

The arms tightened around her. "Stay here for the rest of your life," Andy said. "Stay right here until you really feel okay. And then we're heading right back," he added firmly.

"No," Kim announced flatly. "Not on your life. I'm perfectly all right now. We haven't come this far to just throw in the sponge. What about Pete Madden? What about justice?"

"Right now I don't care as much about Pete Madden, or even about justice, as I care about you. Listen, that guy darned near killed you."

"Us," amended Kim. "Do you suppose it was an accident, or—"

"Assume it was deliberate," Andy said grimly. "Someone could be desperate enough to get us out of the way, desperate enough to kill us."

"Then, if that's true, it means we're getting close to something important. Could that 'something important' be Bill Jones? He's the real threat. Okay, then, all the more reason for us to get to him. Come on. I'm okay, so let's get on with it. Please!"

It wasn't as simple as all that. The car itself was undamaged, but they had a flat tire, burst when it crashed into a rock. Kim started to get out to help change it.

"You stay put," Andy ordered. "Don't you move. I'll do it."

She leaned back, allowing herself the luxury of feeling fragile and protected. She would have resented it and argued hotly if Tom had treated her that way. But this was not Tom.

When the job was done, Andy got behind the wheel and drove cautiously for a mile or so, to test the steering mechanism. Luckily, it seemed to be undamaged.

"I'll make a bargain with you, Kim," he announced. "I'll take you to Santa Elena and park you in a nice, safe hotel, go out to the cabin, get Jones, and pick you up on the way back."

"Oh, no, you don't," she yelped. "If you try, I'll—I'll hire another car and—and beat you there! Just see if I don't!"

As it turned out, Santa Elena was a one-street town that boasted a post office in a grocery store, a gas station, a diner, and no hotel at all.

The postmistress still refused to give out information. The counterman at the diner said yes, he guessed he'd seen the young fella once or twice. He guessed he was staying out at the Saunders shack, about five miles out of town on a dirt road. Didn't make much sense, staying out there with the well dry and all. Had to tote water in buckets and tin cans. "Guess these artist fellas have their own ideas. Kind of funny, though," he added.

"Mr. Saunders," interrupted Kim. "Do you know him?"

"Sure. From the East, New York. Pretty rich, I guess. Bought the place dirt cheap. He thought he'd turn it into a resort area and get even richer. Sure wish it had worked out. Would have brought money to Santa Elena, too. Sure could use it." He described Commissioner Saunders accurately enough for identification.

"Never did hit water when he drilled," the counterman continued. "Finally just gave up and went back East. Didn't bother to try to sell it. Nobody'd buy, so it just sits there, going to pieces."

"How do we get there?" Andy asked.

"Funny thing; this fella Jones acted real surprised when he found Saunders owned the cabin. Didn't bother him, though. Said he'd just accept it. 'No point in making waves,' he said. Funny thing, though, if Saunders was a friend of his, sending him to a place without water."

This could go on all day, Kim thought. Obviously, so few people passed through Santa Elena that the man was anxious to keep any audience he could trap. She knew she shouldn't complain, either, because they had certainly learned more than they'd bargained for. No wonder Commissioner Saunders had chosen a California spot as the place for the recipient of a "grant." He already owned the place.

He also knew how inaccessible it was, how difficult it was to contact anyone. He probably knew that the postmistress had scruples about divulging any "government" information. And he knew he could find out if anyone came to see Bill Jones. That would be easy; he might even have a financial arrangement with this very counterman to phone collect and inform him.

It was awful to wind up suspecting everyone, Kim thought.

Andy finally managed to obtain directions and to escape by promising they'd stop in for a meal and a real talk on their way back. Unfortunately, they had to stop for gas, and the station attendant was another talker. After forever, they were on their way.

They drove five miles and discovered a dilapidated wooden shack. There wasn't a sign of life. An old pickup truck was parked outside, but it looked as if it had expired. They drove on, found no other cabin at all for five more miles, turned around and went back.

"This has to be it," Andy mused. "Guess he might be off somewhere painting. Sure looks lonely, doesn't it?"

"Spooky," Kim said. "Let's look around, though. We've come three thousand miles and gone through a lot. He has to be here, and that's all there is to it." She bounced out of the car and headed for the rickety porch.

"Careful," cautioned Andy, taking her arm. "Some of those floorboards look rotten. I've already had my scare about you and your pretty little neck."

He rapped on the door. There was no answer. "Anybody home in there?" he called.

Nothing.

"Hello in there. Jones, Bill Jones!" Andy shouted.

Silence.

"It can't be the right cabin," Kim said. "We must have missed it somewhere."

Andy turned the doorknob tentatively. He pushed the door. It creaked and swung open. "Hello! Anybody home?"

They stepped into semidarkness. Even in the gloom, they could see they had come to the right place, after all. There were frames of canvas lined up against all four walls of the one-room shack. A big easel loomed in the center of the space.

There was an old-fashioned, pull-down kerosine lantern suspended from the ceiling over a table. Andy jiggled it, nodded satisfaction when it gurgled, removed the glass chimney, turned up the wick, and lighted it with a match. It smoked fiendishly for an instant, until he lowered the wick a bit and put the chimney back in place.

Now they could see the actual paintings. Kim gasped. She was no real connoisseur, but these had to be good, really good. There were boldness and strength to the desert scenes. There was one picture of the water, Long Island Sound, viewed from the rocks at Neadham, painted from memory or brought here from the East. The water looked wet, and even Kim knew this meant real skill on the part of the artist.

Meanwhile, where was the artist?

Andy looked under the bunk bed. Kim, without stopping to think, flung open the doors of the old-fashioned clothespress.

She leaped back, crying out in horror, then flung herself into Andy's arms, shuddering. "Oh, no, no, *no!*" she sobbed. "*No!* Oh—get it away. It—it fell against me—"

"It" was redheaded Bill Jones. There was a bullet hole in the center of his forehead, a gaping hole like a third eye. Kim couldn't bear to look and couldn't stop staring in revulsion.

"Go outside," Andy said, steering her to the door. "Go out and wait in the car."

She couldn't. That would be even worse, being alone and knowing that a murderer was somewhere near. And he must be near. The body was still warm when it touched her. No, she had to stay as long as Andy stayed in here.

Andy knelt down, felt for a pulse, shook his head, and covered the body with a blanket from the bunk. It was better then, but Kim's stomach still churned.

"Why? Why?" she whispered.

"So he won't testify against—against anyone," Andy said bitterly. "They tried to knock us off, then decided to play it safer and get him. Poor guy."

"But who? Who could have done it?"

"It's easy enough to hire a killer if you have the right connections," he said. "It's important to catch the actual killer, too, but even more important to get the guy who ordered it."

"We have to notify the police," Kim said, her voice faint.

Andy was too busy to answer. He was rummaging through papers piled on the table beside a portable typewriter. He tossed them down impatiently, dumped a wastebasket, and began pawing through the contents.

"What—" Kim's breath gave out.

"I'm looking for something, anything. I don't *know* what I'm looking for." Andy fumed. "I'm trying to find anything at all that might be incriminating." He smoothed out a torn and crumpled sheet of paper. "It's a letter to our old buddy, Commissioner Saunders," he said in awe.

"Looks as if he'd torn it pulling it out of the type-writer."

" 'Dear Commissioner Saunders,' " Andy read aloud. " 'There may be a simple explanation to the questions in my mind, but, simple or not, I must ask you to explain.

" 'The grant from the Dier Foundation came as a surprise, out of the blue. It seemed like a miracle, but, even at first, it made me uneasy because I had made no application and had had no interview. I suppose I was afraid to question it, for fear it would go up in smoke. I should have questioned.

" 'I discovered, only after I arrived in Santa Elena, that the cabin offered to me belongs to you. That's when I really began to worry, so I checked the Dier Foundation—called the library in Los Angeles. There is no record of such a foundation.

" 'Okay, Commissioner, who is sending me checks? You? If so, why? You and I were never friends; I was at you all summer to get the rocks at the Neadham Beach sprayed. It was your re-sponsibility to have the spraying done, and a kid was injured because you neglected it.

" 'How come I wind up in your cabin, Com-missioner? Common sense tells me it must have something to do with Pete Madden and his in-jury. Did you get me out of the way so I wouldn't tell someone that you were to blame?

" 'No, I am not accusing—just posing questions. You had better explain, and it had better be good, or I'll write to the mayor of Neadham or the chief of police and ask them a few questions.

" 'Sure, I want a year to paint, but not badly enough to cover for you if what I suspect is true.' " It was signed "William J. Jones."

"He must have retyped it because it tore. Oh, that poor kid," Andy said softly. "That poor innocent kid. He sensed there was something rotten going on, figured Saunders was trying to cover himself, but he didn't have the vaguest idea how bad things were. He practically signed his own death warrant."

Hurrying now, Andy shoved the paper into his pocket, grabbed Kim's hand, and ran with her out to the car. He shoved the ignition key into the switch and revved up, slammed the car into reverse and then into drive. They leaped forward. Then he slammed on the brakes.

"Give me that road map, Kim. Quick!"

"What's the matter? You know the way to Santa Elena. We can phone there."

"No," he said sharply. "We're going to have to skirt the law just a bit and phone in an anonymous tip about the murder. Can't go back to Santa Elena where everybody will recognize us. They know we're from New York. They'll tell the police about us. Someone will stop us at the airport and hold us as material witnesses, maybe for weeks."

"Maybe that's better." The idea horrified Kim, but she believed in the letter of the law. "Isn't that how to—to have the local police backtrack all the way to Saunders, with our help?"

"Criminal mind—I told you I have a criminal mind," Andy muttered. "We have to go back. Come on."

He raced into the cabin, began wiping the doorknob with his handkerchief. Then he stopped, horrified. "What am I thinking of! I can't wipe our prints off without wiping those of the killer. I'd be obstructing—wrong—lose my license to practice—"

The horrible truth dawned on Kim. They, she and Andy, might be accused of the murder. And they couldn't do a thing to protect themselves.

"Come on," Andy urged. "We've got to get out of here. Look at your map. Find me a way out of here, some back lane. We have to find some other town and phone highway patrol. Then I have to call my boss and tell him to take over the Madden trial—in case we don't make it back."

"There's what looks like a sort of road up ahead," Kim said, stabbing a finger on her map. "Try it. It swings to the right and circles back around Santa Elena. There are a couple of little towns—"

"Wait!" Andy held up a hand for silence.

Kim could hear the roar of a car. Distant, coming closer.

Andy took off, screeching the tires, and went barreling down the road in the direction leading away from Santa Elena. Then he turned off and ran the car behind a scrubby growth of tall weeds. He got out and lay down, peering back toward the cabin.

Kim's head began to throb again. Then she remembered to breathe, and the pain eased. The pain transferred to her chest; it felt as if someone were tightening a steel band.

I want to go home, she thought frantically. *I want to go home and find Dad there and tell him everything. He'll know what to do.*

"Let's get out of here," Andy whispered, climbing back into the car and easing it off to a start, almost soundlessly.

"The car," Kim whispered. "Did you see the car? Shouldn't we—get the license number or something?" *Please say no,* she begged inside her head. *I'll try to do what you think is right. I want to go back. Only I don't; I just want to go home.*

"It was a sheriff's car," Andy whispered back. "Do you realize what that means?"

Kim's head was whirling. She couldn't realize anything—except the primitive need to be home.

"It means someone's already called in about the murder," Andy said tightly. "Who? Who else but the guy who did it? And why? To set us up. Maybe he tried to kill us in an accident. Then he did kill Bill Jones, went back, and found we'd escaped. Okay, so he changes his plan. This one's even better; covers him and puts us out of the action completely. In jail. In the gas chamber."

13
if, if, if

"Hang on," Andy ordered. "We're going to head back to the San Bernardino Mountains. It's going to be hairy, but maybe we can drop out of sight long enough—"

"We ought to go back," gasped Kim. She would die if he turned around, but she had to say it.

"I have to get to a phone," Andy said grimly. "Even if they catch up with us, I have to get to a phone first. I still have a responsibility to the Maddens. Have to get my boss to take over. Have to tell him to go into court and get a delay. He can get it—murder of a key witness—"

They roared over a bridge spanning an arroyo. Kim thanked her stars that at least it wasn't the rainy season. Odd even to think of the rains, except that her mind seemed to be producing obstacles to add to the weight of real ones.

Andy fought the wheel, maintaining speed around precipitous turns as they began the climb into the hills. He could really drive, thank heavens, Kim thought as he cut another turn close on the inside.

A town appeared out of nowhere, around a bend. Phone just ahead. Oh, a hex on these awful, glass-walled booths stuck on the side of the road, exposed from every direction!

By now the police might have a description of them and of the car. The counterman and the garageman in Santa Elena could supply the description. Even the postmistress, because now this was "government business," and she was government minded to the core. Oh, yes, she'd probably be the first to volunteer.

She would even remember, and report, that someone from the East had phoned, asking how he could contact William J. Jones. Of course, she would add righteously, she had divulged no such information. But she would even remember the name of the caller, Andrew Hill.

"Hurry," Kim begged as Andy parked and fished for change to summon the operator. "Call collect. Don't stop—" But, of course, he had to have change to institute a collect call.

"Your boss won't be there," she wailed. "There's a three-hour time difference. He won't be at his office. Let me call my father instead!"

"You don't know if he'll be home," Andy reminded her shortly. "My boss has an answering service. If worse comes to worst, and he isn't at the office or at home, I can give the girl the message."

And the girl might be part of the plot, Kim

thought, a bit wildly. Everyone in the world seemed to be involved against them.

That brought up an even more dismaying thought: It wasn't only the police who were looking for them. Somewhere, perhaps right inside a store, looking out at them, there was a murderer who was equally anxious to find them and turn them over to the authorities! *Oh, hurry, Andy! Hurry. Don't just stand there talking! Come* on!

But, of course, he had to talk and talk and talk if his boss was to understand any of it, if he was to get a delay in the Madden trial, find some way to put Saunders under surveillance— and start building some sort of defense for his junior partner and Kim Aldrich.

Something was wrong. Kim could see Andy's face through the glass. He looked as if he were going into shock. He hung up, looking utterly stunned, and, on slow feet that were like lumps of lead, dragged his way back to the car. He climbed in and slumped.

"What is it? What happened?" she begged.

"The Maddens have decided to drop the suit," he said dully.

Kim was outraged. "So, somebody got to them, too! But how? How?"

"Somebody warned the Maddens that they were going to bring the adoption out in court, let the boy know. The parents already know how Duncan MacKenzie can twist things to make them seem like monsters. They already know that he can pull the world out from under Pete, throwing it at him without warning."

It was all wrong. "Look, we have to get back there. We have to talk to them. Pete has to know he's adopted. They're going to have to tell him sooner or later. They have to tell him now, do the telling themselves, gently. Don't you see?"

"My boss said they were adamant. Drop the suit."

"Well, they just can't," Kim said flatly. "That boy is a *child*. He has to grow up and believe in the love and goodness of the people who adopted him and became his parents because they wanted him. He has to believe in law and order and justice because—because *somebody* has to believe, in his generation, or—or the whole country will go down the drain."

She was babbling now, the words gushing out in torrents. "There are so many kooks—so easy for trained people—agents—to take impressionable kids and twist them around. They're crusaders at heart; all kids are. So along comes an agent and gives them a cause, and they think it was all their own idea. They don't know they're puppets dancing on the ends of strings, tearing down the country from within—"

"Okay," Andy said shortly. "We'll make a run for it. See if we can get on a plane, see if we can elude police at the other end, see if we can talk sense into the Maddens, see if—"

If, if, if. What an agonizing word. An insurmountable, utterly dreadful word! If they ever got out of this mess, Kim vowed, she would delete it from her vocabulary.

She clenched her fists until the knuckles showed white. All the way to the airport, she pushed her feet against the floorboards, as if she could make the car go faster. And she kept her eyes closed because she was so terrified of what might happen when they did get there.

Maybe Andy Hill thought his mind would fit a criminal role. Hers wouldn't. She could never stand it, the fear, the running.

"We made it so far," Andy grunted as he pulled into the airport, leaped out, and went to turn in the car keys.

Dear heaven, there was a conspiracy against them. No, the clerk couldn't simply mail the receipt. Certainly not, and it would only call attention to them and waste further time if they asked. Oh, no. The clerk must come out, check the mileage, look the car over for possible damage, write, talk, and thank them forever and ever.

And now they had to find a plane. One leaving *now*. With space for two.

"Maybe we should take different flights," Kim said, appalled at the thought of traveling three thousand miles alone with her thoughts. "I mean—we'd double the chances of someone's getting there—"

"Not on your life," Andy said. "I'm not letting you out of my sight, and that's final."

Bless you, Andy Hill. Kim let out a sigh of relief.

Mercifully or not—depending on what was waiting at the other end—they found a flight that was just leaving. They had to run for it.

They collapsed in their seats. Kim was limp with relief. But she discovered, in the next few hours, that the tension was even worse when there was nothing at all they could do except sit, holding hands, and wait. Kim read over the instructions for the use of the oxygen mask, wondering if she were going to need it, because her heart was pounding so hard.

Amazing that the human body could stand so much without giving out, that the mind could stand such strain without snapping or, as Kim remembered reading in a novel, "going around the bend." She felt as if she were already straining to see around the bend. And then she discovered the answer: sleep.

She opened her eyes and realized they were already in the landing pattern. Andy was still asleep, played out and now recharging his batteries.

"Ready for the next round," she whispered,

shaking him gently, pointing to the SEAT BELTS sign.

He came awake instantly, totally.

"What's the drill?" she asked urgently, wondering how they could have simply slept, without first working out a plan. "Do we split up now? I mean, you drive your car and I—" Intolerable idea. "First—I mean, if we have any choice—I want to call home. I didn't tell anybody about anything, and I want my father—"

"Right," Andy agreed. "After that, I'll take you home in a cab. We can leave both cars here until later."

An ominous word, *later*.

There were all sorts of people waiting to meet the passengers as they came through the exit. At any second, Kim thought, one of them, or two of them, would come over and say quietly, "Police. You're under arrest."

It could be those two clean-cut young men in dark suits. No, they kissed an older woman and called her Mom and asked if she'd had a good trip.

Then, that fortyish man who could fade into a crowd and never be remembered. Like Dan Aldrich, who could leave home looking as neat as a business executive, attaché case and all. And then, with his hat pushed in a bit, tie loosened, coat opened, look rumpled enough to be just anybody or nobody, a tired man leaning against a pillar in Grand Central, reading his paper, waiting for a train. But all the time, watching his suspect.

No. This man was shaking hands with a young serviceman, grinning broadly, pounding him on the back, then fumbling for words, embarrassed, proud.

"Let's go." Andy took her elbow and walked her along the ramp to the terminal. A hundred people followed them.

Andy stopped abruptly and pulled her from the tide. He bent down. "Ladies' room," he whispered. "Don't they have phones in those places? Go inside and call your father. Tell him where you are. Tell him we're leaving right away to go to your home. I'll stand guard while you're inside."

So. Someone *was* following them, someone Andy had somehow spotted. A man, obviously. Police? Maybe so, maybe not, and if not, who? Andy thrust her inside a door. Yes, there was a phone.

She dialed and waited. One ring, eight rings.

"Hello," said Gerta. "Hello, Aldrich residence."

"Gerta, it's me, Kim. Is my father there?" *Please, oh, please!* "Is Tom there? Is *anybody* there?"

"I am here." Gerta was offended.

No time to worry about hurt feelings. "I know,

but is my father there? I have to speak to him."

"Where are you? Is something wrong? Are you calling from California? You said you would be there until—"

"*Please!*" Kim was begging now. "Gerta, my *father.*"

"He phoned just a while ago. He said he would be home for breakfast. I am to fix waffles—"

Morning! Good grief, it was morning. Kim had been too mixed up to realize. It was Sunday morning.

"What time is it now?" Kim demanded. What time would her father be there?

It was six o'clock. He would be there about nine. No, Tom was not at home.

"Gerta, listen," Kim said urgently. "Listen carefully. Tell my father I called from Kennedy Airport. Yes, Kennedy. Tell him six o'clock. Tell him I'm with Andy Hill, a lawyer from Neadham. We're leaving here right now, going straight home from here."

"That is good—" Gerta began.

"Yes. Yes, but, Gerta, in case I don't get there —tell him I'm wearing my blue suit and blue shoes. Blue purse. No hat."

She could picture the headlines, read the copy: *last seen wearing. . . .*

"You calm down, Kim, and listen to me." This was the loving, protective, but occasionally stern Gerta talking. It was her firm belief that a child must learn self-control. She refused to talk to that child until he or she was calm enough to listen. She was still rearing Kim.

"I said your father would be here for breakfast. On Monday. This is Sunday."

Kim groaned.

"You are in trouble, so do not bother to argue. You wait right there. I will come."

Dear Gerta, the avenging angel taking care of her cherub. "No," Kim said gently. "It's better if I leave now and go straight home."

"If you do not come, I will call the FBI," Gerta announced. The FBI was guardian angel, and she didn't hesitate to call if one of her cherubs had a problem. It had been a source of occasional embarrassment for Agent Aldrich.

This was not an FBI case, Kim thought miserably. She only wished it were, with herself somehow safely established on the side of the law.

She said good-bye and hung up, not sure she would ever see Gerta at all, and rushed to rejoin Andy.

He wasn't there! She glanced up and down wildly. He simply was not there.

And now what do I do?

Go home. Just go home and—and hide under the bed or in the closet or in Gerta's arms—or somewhere. Get control of herself and then take it from there, alone. Talk to the Maddens on the phone. Make them agree to appear in court on Monday. For Andy.

For Andy, she thought, sick at heart. Where was Andy? Had he been arrested? Or— How could she find him and help him? She couldn't. There wasn't a chance of finding him in this vast complex. So she had to carry on for him and hope and pray for him.

Kim skittered through knots of people, dashed for the big glass doors. Too many people waiting for cabs. Quicker to go in her own little gun of a TR. She ran through parking lots, past acres of cars, hoping she remembered where she had left hers, so she wouldn't have to stop and find her ticket. Even the ticket would do little good, only give her the number of the lot, not the exact location—and each lot contained hundreds of parking spaces.

Andy; oh, Andy. Her side hurt. She couldn't breathe. Andy.

He had said he loved her. He wouldn't have left by choice. Something must have happened to him. Bill Jones had been murdered, so they weren't afraid to kill. If anything happened to Andy, she couldn't bear it.

There! There it was, right between two big cars. She'd almost run right past her TR because it was so small and low. Keys! Parking ticket so she could pay the fee at the gate and get out of there.

Andy. I'll handle it for you, I promise. And I'll find you. Dead or alive. Oh, no! Alive! Please, alive!

She was standing beside her little car, scrabbling around through the contents of her purse, trying to find the parking ticket. Bending over, peering.

She felt someone behind her, tensed, and planned her judo throw. She'd use it and ask questions later.

Kim never had a chance. She never even knew what hit her.

It was a nightmare. Of course it was, so just wake up and end it. But what a terribly realistic one, so hard to shake off. It was as real as real, and she was twelve years old, on a wheeled stretcher, rolling along to the operating room for an appendectomy. Or was it the time she had fractured her leg?

She was scared, so awfully frightened. They put a mask over her face. She could smell the ether. She was smothering, and didn't anybody care?

Ether.

Now she was floating. How odd to smell the salt water from the operating room. Maybe the hospital was near the ocean. Didn't matter. Too sleepy to care.

Kim didn't know anything at all for quite a considerable time.

14
only
human

Thirsty, always so thirsty when you come from the operating room.

Kim tossed her head fretfully, feeling around on the bedside table for a glass of water. No water. She was almost weak enough to cry about it.

Silly. All you have to do is buzz for a nurse, and she'll bring the water. That is, if you can find the buzzer. Usually right under the pillow, pinned to the sheet so it won't fall to the floor.

Where is the stupid old thing? Must be there somewhere. Okay, so it isn't; you can always yell for a nurse, can't you? Never. Out of character to scream.

Never scream, not if your name's Kim Aldrich. Except—except if you open the door of an old-fashioned clothespress and—and—and a body falls out. Then scream. Scream now!

Her vocal chords were paralyzed. "Andy," she whimpered.

"She's coming out of it," said the nurse. Odd kind of nurse, wearing a greenish something, sweater and skirt or suit. No cap, either. Odd.

"Andy?" Kim was scared to the depths. She could barely whisper.

"Are you feeling better?" asked the gray-haired woman.

"Who are you?" demanded Kim, struggling to sit up, staring around wildly.

For a nightmarish instant she thought she was back in the cabin outside Santa Elena. No, there was no clothespress.

This was different, rough but entirely different. It looked like a fishing shack of some sort. There were rods and tackle carefully stowed on wall racks. A landing net hung from a nail. No electricity. A kerosine lamp stood in the middle of a round dining table. It cast a soft glow.

Kim was lying on a cot. She could smell ether. She could taste it. "I feel sick," she said abruptly.

She was sick. The woman held a basin for her, held her head, then bathed her face with cold water. It felt nice. Then the cold seemed to reach her bones, and she shivered.

The woman covered her with another blanket. Kim wanted to pull it over her head. She didn't, because she had things to do, important things. She'd remember what they were any minute now, as soon as the queasiness passed.

"Who are you? Where am I?" Her voice was stronger now.

"Sh," cautioned the woman. "I'll tell you what little I know, but please be quiet. There's a little boy in the other room, a very frightened little boy. He's asleep now, poor child. Let him sleep."

Things were coming clear. "What little boy?" demanded Kim.

"I don't really know for sure, because he won't say a word. He just stares at me with those huge eyes, like a trapped animal. I don't believe he could talk if he tried. It's a terrible thing to see, just terrible. We've been here together since last night.

"I tried to comfort him. I was frightened enough myself, but he's just a child. He crouched there in his wheelchair. I put him to bed when he collapsed from exhaustion. He cried in his sleep—"

Wheelchair. "Red hair?" Kim interrupted.

"Yes," she answered. "It's the Madden boy? Of course, I assumed it was."

"If I can just get up, I'll go and make sure," Kim said between her teeth. *And then I'll just doggone well find out where* you *figure, whoever you are.*

She was as limp as a dishrag. Her knees were made of spaghetti. She lurched to the table and started to lift the lamp but thought better of it in her weakened condition. It wouldn't do to drop it and set a fire; there were problems enough without that.

"You carry the lamp," she ordered curtly.

The woman led the way to a small room with paneled walls. It was furnished sparsely with a bureau, a straight chair, and an iron bed. There was an Indian rug of some sort on the bare wood floor. A child-sized wheelchair was in the corner.

Pete Madden was a small heap of misery, even in sleep. The covers were partly over his tear-streaked face. One hand crept out from the blankets when the woman held the lamp close.

"Sparky," he whispered. Then he began to cry, without even waking.

Poor little baby! Kim wept inwardly. *Poor defenseless mite.* They didn't even let him have his dog! She smoothed the hair back from his forehead and said softly, hoping to get through to the child without awakening him, "Shh, honey; it's all right. Everything's all right now." After a moment the whimpering stopped.

What was going on? This was not to be tolerated. She would not allow it. And so, Kim decided, she had better get on about the business of ending it. Somehow. She motioned the woman to lead the way back to the other room so they could talk.

"Now, tell me, and you'd better make it good," she said, sitting down on the cot.

That's what Andy had said when he'd found her hiding in the trees near his carriage house. "Tell me and it had better be good." *Oh, Andy,*

*Andy! I'll have to think about you later, because
now I have to—*

"I don't know exactly where to begin," the
woman said.

"Tell me first what day it is and what time."

It was Sunday evening. The woman didn't
know what time it was; she had no watch.

And Kim had lost some twelve hours somewhere. Gerta would be frantic! Gerta would
phone the FBI. And they would tell her to call
the local police. The local police would not take
it too seriously, yet. Not for a day or two.

Well, Dan Aldrich would take it seriously,
that was for sure. Oh, he'd find her, sooner or
later. Dead or alive. Too late to prevent the
Maddens from dropping the suit. Too late, perhaps, to save Andy or Pete or any of them.

"Who are you?" she challenged the woman.

"My name is Marian Casey."

Casey? Casey. John Casey. "The judge's
wife?" Kim asked. Worse and more of it. The
judge himself was involved in this ghastly
thing, a man who sat right under the legend, "In
God We Trust." Equal justice under law! Hah!

The woman nodded.

"So, your husband ordered—" Kim bit off
her accusation that the judge had ordered at
least two kidnappings. And at least one murder—Bill Jones's. Maybe two! *Oh, no! Please,
not Andy. Careful! Don't let the woman know*

how much you know, or you'll never get out of
here alive, never save Pete; and you have to
save him, because there's nobody else to do it.
So you have to stay alive yourself, obviously.

"Now, just a minute," the woman said de-
fensively. "My husband isn't at fault for what
he did—is going to do. It's not his fault at all.
He's not a young man. He's supposed to retire
in two months. He has served on the bench for
more than twenty years and, before that—"

"So now he's going to throw the case." Kim
sneered. "Walk off with a fistful of money. Fine
judge he is. He's a real hero."

It wasn't that way at all, Mrs. Casey protested. He had refused bribe after bribe. No,
this was her fault. She had walked into it blind-
ly. She was afraid, after he had refused the
bribes, frightened to death that they'd harm her
husband. So, when someone came to the house,
said he was a detective, and told her that her
husband had been shot and wanted her, she
didn't even think to ask to see his badge.

"I just grabbed my coat and went with them,"
Mrs. Casey admitted. "There were actually two
of them, one out in the car, the driver. They
drove around and around, all over the county,
up around the Kensico Reservoir, over to the
Hudson, into the Connecticut backcountry,
near the Sound. I tried to keep track. . . ." Her
voice faded.

"Then what?" prompted Kim.

"Then they stopped somewhere and took me into a house and told me to telephone my husband. He was home by then and frantic with worry about me. I told him they said I could go back to him as soon as the trial was over." She covered her face with her hands, muffling her voice. "I wanted to tell him not to listen to them, to see that justice—"

Mrs. Casey looked at Kim, pleading for understanding. "I couldn't do it. I was—frightened. Not only for myself, but for him. John and I are so close, and we have only this little time until we retire and go to Florida. We already have a house there. It wouldn't be fair to make him go alone. I'm—so ashamed."

And so human, thought Kim sadly. And, no doubt, the judge was only human, too. "Everyone has his Achilles' heel," Andy had said. "Who would risk the life of his wife or the girl he loved?" The thought of Andy was a knife.

"Well, then," Kim said in a businesslike tone, "once the case is over and you're safely home, he'll report your kidnapping to the FBI. Then the Maddens' lawyer can appeal the case and—"

"He's not a young man," Mrs. Casey whispered. "He's too old for that kind of fight, too tired. It's too dangerous. No. If I ever get home, we're going to retire immediately. I can't help it. We're both too old—"

She began to shudder violently. "I have to make these people believe it, too. If I don't— well, don't you see? If they think there's one chance my husband would— Well, they'd never let him get away with it."

"Who are 'they'?" Kim asked.

"I don't know. I honestly don't know."

All right, then, what did she know about Pete Madden being brought here? And where, incidentally, was "here"? Did she know?

"We're on an island, that much I do know. I tried to keep track of where we were going. I'm not sure, but I think this might possibly be one of the Thimble Islands. They're right near Greenwich, Connecticut. They're rather unusual, you know."

Kim didn't know.

"They're privately owned," Mrs. Casey explained. "Families with considerable money own their own islands. The men go ashore by boat and commute to New York on the New Haven. The wives and children sort of rough it, get back to nature. No electricity, no phones. There's a story that this area used to be a pirate hideaway and that some of Morgan's treasure is hidden on one or another of the Thimbles. Of course, we may not be there at all."

Islands, boats. Kim's heart leaped. If there were a boat, she'd find it!

"They brought me here by boat and just left

me," Mrs. Casey went on. "They told me there was food, fuel for that crazy heating contraption that scares me to death, lamps. But no phone. And no boat. They told me not to bother about looking for a boat, that they'd checked to see that there were none."

If they had to check to find out, then they didn't own the island, Kim reasoned. "Well, then, someone's going to investigate to see why there are lights. The owners must have notified the Harbor Patrol or the Coast Guard when they closed up for the winter."

No, Mrs. Casey said. The shutters were all closed. She had been warned not to show any lights. She had been very careful.

As for Pete, she went on, the boy had been brought later, kicking and biting, fighting like a little tiger. They had shoved him inside the cottage and told him to mind Mrs. Casey, and that was the story of Pete. He hadn't said a word or eaten a mouthful, poor little tyke.

"Sh!" Kim held up her hand for silence. Someone was coming. Okay, she had missed her chance with her judo back at Kennedy. This time she would be ready.

So what if she was still feeling a bit wobbly? It didn't matter as long as she kept her cool. Judo was technique, not strength, the calculated means of using the opponent's very weight and strength against him. Throw him off-balance, and then help him fall the rest of the way. Hard. Chop him in the bridge of the nose if you have to finish him off. Not that she'd be able to go that far, but she could—must—throw him hard enough to put him out of action for a nice long time. Then go for the boat. If there was a second man in the boat— Well, she'd worry about that when the time came.

"Wait!" Mrs. Casey gasped.

Wait yourself, thought Kim grimly, *you— you collaborator*. She clamped her hand over the woman's mouth and warned, "You make one peep and, so help me, you'll be more afraid of me than of those men. I mean it."

The woman's eyes bugged. She opened her mouth when Kim let her go, but no sound came out.

Kim took up her position, pressed against the wall, so that when the door opened, she could grab the wrist attached to the hand on the knob. Then she would put out her foot, pull the man forward with a hard yank, and, presto, roll him right over her hip and send him flying.

Easy, when your opponent is your dad or your brother. If you flub it, they give you a second chance. This was a one-shot, and if she failed, the answer would probably come from a gun.

It worked. A body hurtled across the room,

crashed against the far wall, and slumped in an awkward pile on the floor.

"Quick," Kim ordered, faint now with relief. "Find something to tie him with, fishing line, anything. Quick, he's only stunned."

"I think he broke his arm when he landed," Mrs. Casey whispered.

"Serves him right," Kim said grimly. "Come on, help me tie him with something. Then I'll see about a boat, come back and get you and Pete—"

Pete. The crash must have awakened him. She had to get this tying job done instantly, then go to him and tell him everything was going to be all right, that he was going home.

Fishing line—nylon line. She tore at it frantically, trying to remove it from a reel. "Knife," she ordered. "Find me a knife."

And at last she was kneeling beside the limp form. "Hold the lantern so I can make sure the knots are—"

"His arm is broken," repeated Mrs. Casey.

It was indeed, Kim realized, sickened. Andy Hill's arm was broken, and Andy Hill was still unconscious.

15
moonlight
swim

Andy groaned.

"I tried to tell you," said Mrs. Casey. "They brought him here with you. He pretended to be still unconscious from the ether. They gave it to him, too. But he was awake, trying to discover where both of you were being taken. He said they brought him in the trunk of a car. He didn't know you were there until they dumped him into the boat beside you."

"Kim!" Andy's eyes opened. "Thank the Lord you're all right."

He shifted his weight and managed to support his left elbow with his right hand. "Listen, quick. Take hold of my left hand. Now put your other hand under my elbow. Rotate it and then give it a yank. Shoulder's dislocated. Pops out once in a while. Did it first when I was a kid, wrestling. Come on, quick. Yank hard before the swelling sets in."

Kim set her teeth and did it. His face went white. Then the color began to return. "Andy, oh, Andy, darling, I'm so sorry." She put her arms around him.

"Boy, for a little slip of a girl, you sure pack a wallop." He gave a lopsided grin.

"I'm so sorry—"

"I'm the one who's sorry. Kim, I must have rocks in my head. Remember back at Kennedy when I was standing guard while you phoned your dad? Well, I saw someone suspicious, so I decided to lead him away from you. Walked right into a trap. Someone slugged me right in the gut and again across the throat. Walked me, half dragged me, right out of the terminal."

That someone had put Andy's arm over his shoulder and talked, indulgently, as if to an inebriated friend. Andy had been unable to talk at all. Before his strength returned, someone had clamped a cloth over his face, out in the parking lot. That was all he knew until he regained consciousness inside the trunk.

After he and Kim had been deposited in the cabin, and he had made sure she was alive, he had left her in Mrs. Casey's care and gone off to investigate. There were no boats on the island. No guards, either, but they were prisoners.

"Then I'll just have to swim ashore and get help," Kim announced.

"You will do no such thing! The water's like ice; you wouldn't last three minutes. It's dark, and you'd lose your sense of direction. If you reached shore, by some miracle, you'd probably find our guards right there, armed."

"It's worth a try."

"If there's any swimming to be done, I'll do it," Andy said flatly.

Kim was equally stubborn. "You can't. You have a bum shoulder, thanks to me," she said forlornly.

"Okay, then; go find me something to bandage it with. Then we'll give another look around, see if we can find a life jacket, something to use for a raft, oars. Something."

Kim located the kitchen, a primitive affair with a kerosine stove, an icebox, and a sink with a pump. On an open shelf, she discovered another lamp and a red checkered tablecloth. She cut the cloth with a knife and bound Andy's shoulder.

A muffled sob reached them. "Pete!" Kim said, lighting the extra lamp. "He's awake." They hurried in to him.

"I want to go home." The voice came from under the covers.

"You're going home, Pete, just as soon as we can get you there," Andy said. "It'll take a little time, but you be patient, and we'll get you home."

A small face appeared, then vanished beneath the blankets. "No," wailed Pete. "I'll never go home because they—they don't want me."

"Oh, now, honey," Kim said, wanting to cry herself as she gathered the boy in her arms.

"Of course they want you; they love you very much."

"No, they don't," he sobbed, burying his face against her shoulder. "I'm adopted. They didn't think I knew, but I did. I knew for a long time. I—know they don't want me, and they sent me away. But I want Sparky. He's mine; you gave him to me."

"Of course you can have Sparky," soothed Kim, "but you're going home. Believe me, Pete; trust me."

"They don't want me. They *made* me go away."

Oh, no, no, no. He had it all wrong. So Kim Aldrich told him what he should have been told a long time ago, that his parents had chosen him. This, she pointed out, was even better than being a natural child, when parents have to take what's born to them. Pete's mother and father had chosen him, out of all the other children.

He didn't believe her. He insisted his parents had sent him away. They had even packed his suitcase and told him he had to leave.

However that had been managed, she hadn't the faintest idea. But she knew they had to get Pete back home—and soon. How?

"Stay with Mrs. Casey for a little while, Pete. She'll take care of you," she said. "We'll be back after a bit, and then we'll all go home."

A promise to a child was a literal thing. How were they going to honor it? There seemed to be no way. Andy was right; swimming to shore would be next to impossible in the frigid water. There wasn't a trace of a boat anywhere.

And then, in a shed off the kitchen, Kim found a set of fins—and a face mask. Skin diving gear. There had to be a wet suit around!

And there was! Andy yelped with glee when he dragged it from an old wooden chest. In a wet suit, a swimmer could stay in cold water for ages, because the suit provided insulation and kept in body heat.

"That settles it," Andy gloated. "Shoulder or no shoulder, I'm going."

Kim took the suit from him and held it up against him. "Not a chance. It's a girl's suit, or a young boy's. I'm the one, because I'm the only one who can get into it."

"You're not going alone!" Andy was adamant.

They wasted valuable time arguing hotly. In the end, they collected their wits enough to keep looking until they found the top half of another wet suit, one that would fit Andy. It would have to do.

They explained their plan to Mrs. Casey, then peeled to their skivvies, Kim in the kitchen, Andy in the shed. There was only one pair of fins, Kim-sized. She hung them over her arm for the trek in darkness to the water's edge, then put them on and backed into the water so they wouldn't go slap-slap and alert anyone within earshot.

Kim was sure, now, that this was Long Island Sound. The lights on the far side had to be Long Island. Lights on the near shore had to be in Westchester or Connecticut.

Nearby, had she thought? The nearest point of land seemed a million miles away. Between lay the great expanse of black water, ice-cold water that numbed her hands and her heels.

The sky was black and ominous, too. No trace of a moon. She had a horrible thought: Suppose they reached shore, even found help. How would they be able to direct a rescue party back to their Thimble Island, if that's what it was? How would they know which island?

"Ready?" Andy asked softly. "Wow, this is brutal."

"Can you make it?" Kim was worried, to put it mildly. With no protection for his legs, he could easily cramp up. Would she have the strength to tow him, when she wasn't sure she could get there alone?

"Have to," he said shortly.

Have to, she echoed to herself. If he needs a carry, she'd rely on her Red Cross lifeguard training.

"Easy," Andy cautioned. "Breaststroke, side-stroke, backstroke to conserve strength."

"I can swim a crawl without making a sound." He could, too, of course. Good heavens, Andy had grown up in Hawaii. He'd be a powerful swimmer. Well, okay, she was no slouch herself.

They struck out for the nearest light. It never seemed to come closer. One, two, three; one, two, three; one, two, three— She counted her kick beat until it was a metronome in her head. One, two, thr—

"Okay, I give up," she gasped, keeping her voice low. "Have to rest."

There was no answer.

Oh, heaven help me, Kim thought, fighting back panic. *I said I could keep up, but he's from Hawaii, six-beat crawl, a mile away by now. Oh, stupid, stupid. Red Cross says swim breaststroke, head out of the water, to keep your eye on someone.*

Worse, he had only half a wet suit. Cramps. He could have drowned. He'd go down and—

It was all she could do to keep from shouting his name at the top of her lungs. "Andy?" she said softly. "Andy?" Oh, softly, so the sound wouldn't carry to shore, to a guard who might be waiting just in case they tried an escape.

"Kim?"

Had she imagined it? Where was that voice coming from? Water did strange things, bounced back sound, made it seem to come from different directions. Minds did strange things, too.

"Over here," she answered.

The water was Andy Hill's natural habitat. He found her.

"Okay, slow and easy this time, Kim," he said, beside her. "I mean it. Want to rest first?"

"I'm all right." Everything was all right so long as he was there. "How're you doing? How's your shoulder? Your legs?"

"Sure isn't like the blue green waters of home," he answered. "Hey, wait . . . engine. . . ."

Kim had thought it was the pounding of her own heart. Her mind was too numb with cold —cold that traveled from her bare hands, up her arms, to her head—to think. A boat—

She thought she would just come unglued and cry. It was no use, no use at all. They had tried so hard—from New York to Los Angeles to Santa Elena and back. From Kennedy Airport to here. Knocked out, anesthetized, marooned. No sleep, no food for hours—and now, now— It just wasn't fair.

"Down you go," Andy said curtly. "Dive."

She went into the blackness, held her breath until her lungs were bursting, until she lost all perspective and didn't know which way was up. It was a terrifying experience, knowing she had to breathe, not knowing how to surface. Forcing herself to relax and float up.

There was nothing more they could do, she thought hopelessly. If they'd had scuba gear so they could have traveled underwater, maybe they could have made it. No use.

She came up in the beam of a searchlight. A hand reached out for her. She took it, too tired to fight any longer. Apparently Andy felt the same way. He, too, accepted the hand and was pulled up into the boat.

Someone threw blankets around them. They were handed steaming mugs of coffee. Okay; the condemned man and woman ate—drank— a hearty meal.

"If these were the old days, I'd ship you off to a convent for safekeeping," rasped someone who came out of the cabin.

"Dad!" Now Kim knew she'd gone around the bend. "How did *you* get here?"

"I might ask the same of you," he stated. "In fact, I'll insist on knowing, when I get over being so furious. Kim! Kim! You're enough to scare the heart out of the old man." His voice broke.

He cleared his throat. "Now that the pieces are beginning to fit together, though, I'm mighty proud of you."

"Whatever that means," she murmured, completely confused. "How did you find us?"

"Gerta called the FBI."

"But—"

"Yes, I know. Gerta has called the FBI many times, such as when you arrived home late from a kid birthday party or the movies, and so on. But this time, thank the Lord, she did call, and they got a message to me. You've done some harebrained things in your day, but you never before pulled a stunt like telephoning to admit you were in trouble and then not showing up— and no more word from you!"

Dan Aldrich had checked out her entire time since she had left home Saturday morning.

Saturday? Was it only Saturday when she left? It seemed like years.

He had checked with her former roommate and found she hadn't appeared and wasn't expected. He had routed out Mr. Rydell and picked his brains until he knew quite a bit about the Madden suit. He had learned of Bill Jones. He had checked the auto rentals and the mileage on their car. The mileage was close enough for the trip to Santa Elena and back. And he had learned the fate of Bill Jones.

"You shouldn't have run away from there, Kim," he said sternly. "You know better than that. You could have sent word to me. You should have trusted me to— Well, you know better. You, too, Counselor," he snapped at Andy.

"I'm sorry," Kim said meekly. "I—panicked."

"I—guess I did, too, sir," said Andy.

Next, Dan Aldrich informed them, a call had come in from Judge Casey, reporting the kidnapping of his wife. Things began to add up. Kim's disappearance was also classified as a kidnapping, and a full-scale investigation was mounted.

The Maddens were checked out. The boy turned up missing. Two alert teen-agers reported seeing a strange car near the water, with what they supposed was a sack of camping gear, but which could have been a body dumped into a boat. They reported to the local police. A routine FBI check of police headquarters added this information to the kidnapping file.

A runabout was found, hidden on the shore. Kim's handbag was under the bow seat. Soon after that, Agent Aldrich was aboard a Harbor Patrol cruiser, fishing his daughter out of the drink.

Kim had a hysterical desire to laugh. He had done more than just save her and Andy from freezing, she thought. He had saved them from the awkward experience of padding through the streets of some town, barefoot in cold weather, clad in pieces of wet suits, asking to be directed to the police station—and probably being carted off to the funny farm.

"Dad," she said instead, "we've got to go get Pete Madden and the judge's wife."

"Where? Which island?"

Kim didn't have the faintest idea. She was all turned around and had lost her sense of direction completely.

"Describe the cottage," ordered a uniformed officer tersely.

Kim and Andy contributed every scrap of knowledge they had between them.

"Good. That's the Keenely place, I think," he said.

They were there in moments. Strange, when it had seemingly taken hours to swim the distance. They went ashore, Kim and Andy still swathed in blankets, an officer lighting the way.

It was the cottage. But no one was inside. Pete and Mrs. Casey had already been taken away.

16
witness
for the
plaintiff

"No," Kim said flatly. This was just too much.

She was cold and wet and tired and hungry. So was Andy. They had gone through enough for a lifetime within the span of less than two days.

They had flown a total of six thousand miles, wondering if they would be alive from one minute to the next. They had nearly met death when a car sideswiped them and tried to push them over an embankment.

They had driven to a deserted cabin and found it was not totally deserted. Kim had opened a door and the body of a young man, still warm, had fallen out against her.

They had eluded the police and probable arrest in order to come back East and produce proof of complicity, if nothing more, on the part of Commissioner Saunders. They had been kidnapped; they had escaped; they had swum in freezing water.

It would have all been worthwhile, every bit of it, if it had resulted in the rescue of a small crippled boy and a woman.

But now Pete and Mrs. Casey were gone.

"It's my fault," Kim said dully. "I was the one who insisted on swimming ashore. I didn't stop to think. All I did was make things a thousand times worse."

"They" had obviously discovered that Kim and Andy were gone. Now they would know the net was closing in around them. They would take no further risks; they couldn't afford to let Pete or Mrs. Casey go—ever.

They hadn't even bothered to take Pete's wheelchair. He wasn't going to be needing it.

A vivid picture flashed through her mind. It was more real than anything that had happened to her: Pete Madden and Mrs. Casey, floating in the Sound.

"Steady on, skipper," Andy said, putting an arm around her. "Go into the kitchen and put on your dry clothes before you catch your death. First things first."

He changed in the shed. Together, they went back to the living room.

Amazingly, there they were: Pete and Mrs. Casey! Two pairs of terrified eyes stared dumbly. Mrs. Casey's arms were around the child, trying to shield him.

"Tell them, Kim," Dan Aldrich said. "Tell them who I am, that everything's all right. We found them hiding outside. They heard the cruiser and thought—"

Kim could well imagine what they'd thought. "It's all right," she told them. "It's all right. It's over. We're all safe. This is my father. He's an FBI agent. The boat you heard was the Harbor Patrol."

Some of the terror faded from the two pairs of eyes.

"Is he really an FBI agent?" Pete asked, awed. When Kim nodded, he said, "Can I go and live with you?"

She hugged him. "Wouldn't you rather go home?"

"They don't want me. Get Sparky and let me live with you, because otherwise—otherwise I don't have any place to go. . . ."

There was only one possible way of curing his fixation. Take him to his parents and prove how wrong he was. Oh, those poor people, frightened out of their wits, not knowing where Pete was. And poor Judge Casey.

"Can't we phone on the ship-to-shore or the radio or something," she begged, "just so they'll know?"

"It's already done," said Dan Aldrich. "Is everyone all set? Let's go, then. The cruiser is waiting."

A kind pilot took Pete up on the flying bridge and even let him handle the wheel, with a bit of guidance. That brightened his spirits, if only temporarily. When he was carried ashore, how-

ever, he balked at getting into an unmarked
car.

"You're not cops," he accused, struggling to
get free. "That's no cop car. It's a trick. It's all
a trick. Miss Aldrich, please! You promised! You
said I could have Sparky, and now they're taking me away again. Don't let them!" he cried out
in desperation.

"It's all right, Pete; it's all *right*. Dad, can't
you scare up an official car, siren and all, just
to—"

Dan Aldrich vetoed the idea. He wanted to
get the boy and the judge's wife to their homes
as quickly and quietly as possible, then post
guards and have them escorted to court in the
morning.

"Oh, Dad, no! Surely they don't have to go to
court after all they've been through. Couldn't
they get a delay? And, anyway," she just remembered, "the Maddens wanted to drop the
suit, so a delay—"

"Believe me, this is one time they wouldn't
want to miss being in court. And that goes for
you and Andy Hill, here, too. Andy, your boss,
Charlie Tully, is an old buddy of mine from
way back. He's been doing a little investigating
on his own. He's cooked up a few surprises for
tomorrow," Dan Aldrich said, smiling with grim
satisfaction.

And, incidentally, he added, there would be a

guard for one Andy Hill, whether he liked it or not. He didn't, but neither did he object.

None of this made any sense to Pete Madden or comforted him one iota. He clung to Kim, said he was afraid, and refused to go inside his house unless she went with him. Andy went, too, pushing the boy in the wheelchair, which an officer removed from the trunk.

Once inside his home, Pete could no longer doubt whether or not his parents loved him or wanted him. Mrs. Madden broke down and wept as she held her son in her arms. Mr. Madden, tears streaming down his face, put his arms around both of them. Kim and Andy slipped out without anyone noticing. A guard remained, also unnoticed.

When they reached the Casey home, the judge's wife turned to Kim and said, "I'm ashamed that I asked my husband to go against his principles. I hope you won't think too badly of me. I do want to thank you for—" Her eyes were shining. "I'm so proud, proud of my husband, proud of the court, proud of the FBI— proud of people!"

It sounded nice. For entirely too long, it seemed to Kim, the whole world had appeared to be involved in a giant conspiracy against everything that was decent.

They dropped Andy off last, at his carriage

house at the end of a lonely spit of land. He tilted Kim's chin and kissed her, then shook hands with her father.

"See you tomorrow in court, Counselor," said Dan.

Kim was asleep before they reached New York. Once home, she somehow made her way to bed and fell into complete oblivion until morning.

When she awoke in familiar surroundings, she thought she had dreamed the entire thing. Then the horror swept over her again. It was real, every last bit of it. And it wasn't over yet, just because she was home.

Her father drove her to White Plains, hustled her in through the back entrance of the court-house and into a room that was set apart from the courtrooms. Andy was already there and introduced her to his boss, Mr. Tully. Mrs. Casey and the three Maddens were there, also.

"We want to put you on the stand, Kim," Andy said. "Witness for the plaintiff."

It could mean her job, testifying for the op-posing side. Well, she had already risked her life several times for the opposition, so she nodded.

"Wait here, please, all of you, until just the last minute before the doors close. The Maddens will go to the front of the room, of course, but I want the rest of you to sit in the very back. Go in quietly and attract as little attention as possible," Mr. Tully instructed.

Kim was not the first witness. Andy called a Sister Josephine. A sprightly little nun responded, took the oath, and sat on the witness stand.

Under questioning, she unfolded an amazing story. She was affiliated with a foundling home in Chicago. One of her charges had been an infant, Peter Gallagher, whose parents had been killed instantly in a car accident. No adult relatives were found, with the exception of a frail grandmother in Ireland. She was unable to send for the child at that time.

Counsel for the defense objected; this had nothing to do with—

Overruled.

"Meanwhile," continued the nun serenely, "there was a couple anxious to adopt a little boy —a Mr. and Mrs. Madden. They were unable to have a natural child.

"I suggested that they take Peter as a foster child. They were reluctant, because he was not up for adoption. They feared they would grow to love him, and, one day, he would be taken from them."

Peter, she explained, was a sickly infant. She felt he needed love and attention. She appealed to the Maddens to take him for just a month, to build up his strength. And then another month.

And parenthood came so naturally to Mr. and Mrs. Madden that, month by month, they continued to care for Peter.

"I believed that if we all had sufficient patience and faith, the Lord would make them a legal family," the nun said. "However, the Maddens left town suddenly, took Peter with them, and left no trace."

There was a gasp from Mrs. Madden as she reached for her husband's hand.

"I had no way to contact them until a curious thing occurred. A stranger appeared one day and said he was looking for the missing heir to a fortune. It was Mr. Saunders. He said he had reason to believe the heir might be a Peter Madden, but he must check the particulars of the boy's adoption."

So that was it, Kim thought. Pete was not yet adopted. And the Maddens were terrified of having the fact known, believing Pete might be taken from them. They had even dropped the suit rather than have the facts brought to light in court.

"I had certain reservations, so I asked the man's name and phone number," the nun continued. "I said I would pray for guidance and let him know whether or not I felt free to provide any information. I suppose he did not consider further subterfuge necessary. But I had no intention of telling anyone anything without consulting the Maddens. I checked Mr. Saunders' area code, located the town, and learned that the Maddens live in Neadham. I came to Neadham."

Kim wasn't sure what it proved, except that Saunders had been digging for ammunition. The commissioner's neck turned a dull red. He was in the front row. Kim saw his reaction.

"Thank you, Sister. Your witness, Counselor."

"No questions," snapped Duncan MacKenzie.

"I call Miss Kimberly Anne Aldrich to the stand," said Andy.

Commissioner Saunders spun around and stared. Perhaps he could accept the mysterious reappearance of Pete Madden with relative calm, even the unexpected arrival of Sister Josephine, but he was not prepared for Kim. His face turned gray.

Andy elicited from her a description of the beach at Neadham as it had been when she had seen it before the accident. Saunders relaxed, but only for an instant.

Then Andy led Kim into a recital of her trip West. He had her read the torn and crumpled original of a letter from Bill Jones.

"Objection!" roared Duncan MacKenzie. "There is no reason why a person with philanthropic leanings should not choose to remain anonymous when he provides assistance. It has no bearing on—"

Overruled.

Where had she found the letter? Andy asked. In a cabin inhabited by William J. Jones, former chief lifeguard at Neadham.

A cabin owned by Commissioner Saunders? "Objection. Witness has no proof."

Sustained. It didn't matter, really.

And now Andy pounced. When had the witness last seen William Jones? On Saturday last —with a bullet hole in his forehead.

"What?" shouted Saunders, leaping to his feet. "What do you mean, a bullet hole? I never said to kill him, only to keep him out of sight. All right! You can accuse me of a lot of things, but not murder. I had nothing to do with murder!"

Once his control had snapped, he ranted compulsively. He volunteered information as to how, for years, he had taken town funds from the turnstiles. He needed extra funds because he intended to campaign for the office of mayor.

At first, he admitted, he was uneasy about the suit but decided he could turn it to his advantage and emerge a hero. It would be brought out in testimony, in the judge's charge to the jury, that paying off would increase taxes. The citizens would vote him into office on those grounds.

Oh, the arrogance of the man, thought Kim,

stealing from the town, then expecting to be elected mayor by the very citizens from whom he had stolen!

"And you can't accuse me of kidnapping, either," stormed Saunders. "It was their idea—and there was no reason to take the kid."

"Whose idea?" prompted the judge softly.

"Syndicate," snapped Saunders. "You know perfectly well there is organized crime in this county; numbers, horses. Yes, I covered for them. Why not, when they were willing to contribute to my campaign fund? And they agreed to keep track of certain nosy individuals, keep them out of the way until the trial was over. But I didn't tell them to kill anyone. You can't—"

The judge could and did. "Book him," he said.

17
common
cause

The trial was over. Counsel for the plaintiff approached the bench and requested that the suit be officially dropped. A settlement had been agreed upon between the plaintiff and the town of Neadham in the amount of ten thousand dollars.

"A formal charge of murder has been made against the man who shot Bill Jones," Dan Aldrich told Kim as they all filed out of court. "He was apprehended. You and Andy might have to testify in a murder trial, but it won't hurt you. Saunders is charged as an accessory. We'll get him on the kidnapping."

Everyone was milling around in the hall, trying to talk to the Maddens. Kim pushed through the crowd because there was something she had to know.

"They're not going to take Pete away—" she began.

"No," Sister Josephine said. "I came to tell the Maddens that their way is clear now to adopt Peter legally. His grandmother died. He has no other living relatives."

Kim was still puzzled by a number of things. Why, for instance, had the Maddens ever brought suit, when they wanted to go unnoticed? Hadn't they realized that their entire background would be combed for whatever could be used against them?

No, they hadn't realized.

"It wasn't for the money," Mrs. Madden said, reddening painfully. "I felt guilty, so terribly guilty. I thought I wasn't a fit mother. I thought I never should have taken Pete in the first place. I knew I had no right to take him away from Chicago. And then I blamed myself for letting him get hurt. I—I thought if a jury said the town was guilty, then I might believe it myself. And the money might make up to Pete. . . . Then these men came with a gun and took him away, and I thought I'd lost him forever. . . ."

"We've arranged for Pete to go to one of our rehabilitation centers," Mr. Rydell broke in. "No, son, don't worry; we're not going to take you away, just send you to a sort of school several days a week. A place where you'll learn special exercises, so you can walk again soon."

That was just about it. Most of the questions had been answered, most of the problems solved. One major question, however, remained.

Kim and Andy. How did they feel about each other?

She gazed at him, suddenly shy.

"Sir, do you mind if I abscond with your secretary for the rest of the day?" he asked Mr. Rydell.

"Fair enough. She's earned time off," her boss replied. "Just make sure she reports for work tomorrow. No more trips to California. Not on my time, at least."

"Mr. Aldrich? Can you spare your daughter?"

"See that you bring her home early," said Dan, like an old-fashioned father.

Kim and Andy drove, in Victoria, out to the beach where they had met. It was wild and wonderful and deserted.

They sat on the pier, looking out at the Sound, watching the gulls wheel and dip. A pair of ducks drifted past. They didn't talk for a long time.

"Saunders," Kim said at last. "Warped. Warped mind. At least the bench wasn't warped. Judge Casey believes in equal justice under law."

"Mm, forgot to tell you. Judge Cranston is okay, too. Honest—a crusader. My boss went to see him. He had a real heart attack. As for the high figure he set, the half million, well, he had his reasons. They were darned good ones if you ask me.

"A small sum would hardly make the newspapers. A half a million made headlines on page one. That put a real squeeze on Saunders, called a lot of attention to him, packed the courtroom."

So, mused Kim, Saunders had been forced to brazen it out. His twisted mind, contemptuous of ordinary mortals and their rights, had really believed that everything would come out in his favor.

That was about the size of it, Andy agreed. Cranston had had another objective, beyond bringing corruption out in the open so the public would vote the guilty person or persons out of office. He wanted to call attention to the dangerous situation at the beach. It wasn't enough merely to rope off the rock area; it should be decked in with concrete and made safe and usable.

The public would vote for such expenditure of town funds, now that the spotlight was on the area.

"Judge Cranston almost sealed our fate," Kim reminded him.

"That was something even he couldn't have anticipated," Andy said, defending a fellow legal eagle. "Anyway, it was really our own fault we took such a—"

"Such a miscalculated risk," Kim put in.

They were quiet again.

Andy took her hand at last. "What about us?"

"I—don't know. Andy, I don't know. Maybe I'm just too tired to think. I was sure I was in love, but now I wonder if it was just the sharing of a common danger, a common cause."

"One way to find out," he murmured, pulling her into his arms.

Her heart leaped. The kiss was the kind to lead to others, but Kim drew back, carefully, regretfully.

"Let's—let's just not rush things for a while. Let's sort of wait and see how it works out. If what we have is real, it'll grow."

"Come on. I'll take you home so you can sleep on it. Right now my resistance is sort of low, so it's home for you."

He stood up, held out a hand, and pulled her to her feet. He grinned down at her. "Come on, Victoria's waiting."

"I must have rocks in my head." She laughed. "No girl in her right mind would let you get away, not even for a minute. I might regret this to the end of my days."

"I'll be around," Andy promised.

Whitman CLASSICS and ANTHOLOGIES

Black Beauty

Little Women

Heidi

Heidi Grows Up

Tom Sawyer

Huckleberry Finn

The Call of the Wild

Treasure Island

Alice in Wonderland

The Wonderful Wizard of Oz

Famous Fairy Tales

Algonquin: The Story of a Great Dog

Tales of Poe

SHORT STORY COLLECTIONS

A Batch of the Best (Stories for Girls)

Like It Is (Stories for Girls)

Shudders

Golden Prize

That's Our Cleo! *(New)*

Way Out *(New)*

Whitman NOVELS FOR GIRLS

Spirit Town

Gypsy From Nowhere

The Family Name

True to You

Practically Twins

Make-Believe Daughter

The Silver Seven

Bicycles North! *(New)*

Whitman ADVENTURE and MYSTERY Books